MURDER AT

The Complete

BLACK MASK ®

Cases of Tony Key

Volume 1: 1937–38

STEVE FISHER

introduction by John Wooley

illustrations by Joseph A. Farren
and Arthur Rodman Bowker

cover by J. George Janes

BLACK MASK

2024

Table of Contents

Going Hollywood

by John Wooley

THE GOLDEN AGE of Hollywood began, more or less, in the late 1920s, after the movies began to talk and quickly gave notice they weren't about to shut up. That starry-eyed era effectively ended a couple of decades later, after a landmark antitrust case, *The United States v. Paramount Pictures, Inc.,* reached the Supreme Court. In its May 1948 ruling, the Court decreed that the defendants, which included all of Hollywood's major studios, had to divest themselves of the theaters they owned.

That ruling also ended the practice of block booking, in which an independent exhibitor—one whose movie house was not studio-owned—would have to rent a number of other pictures from a major in order to get the features he or she really wanted. Essentially, the Court's decision dismantled the vertically integrated method of producing, booking, and distributing films that had been the backbone of the motion-picture industry for years; this, coupled with the specter of television peeping over the horizon, was enough to destroy the long-lived "studio system" of hiring talented people, putting them on payroll, and bringing them along—often via lower-budgeted B-pictures made right on the big-studio lots—to see which ones might show that intangible quality it took to become a star.

Long before the studio system came tumbling down, however, the name "Hollywood" had become synonymous with magic and escapism, turning out celluloid dreams in all conceivable sizes and shapes, acted out by the closest thing America had to royalty. And, as is usual when dealing with royalty, whispers of erotic excesses and other scandals swirled around the larger-than-life icons who moved across the nation's screens, providing counterpoint to the reams of hagiographic copy offered up by the fan mags and studio publicity machines.

To the average American, movie-industry people, from stars right down to grips, were unusual, intriguing, and exotic, larger-than-life symbols of something beyond an existence that too often embraced the mundane, or worse—especially in those Depression Era years that formed the first part of the movies' Golden Era. Hollywood provided a means of escape.

And so did Hollywood fiction.

For my money, two of the best early Tinseltown novels are the wonderfully boozy and acerbic *Queer People* (1930), by the brothers Carroll and Garrett Graham, and Edgar Rice Burroughs' *The Girl from Hollywood*, (which features a dope-addict subplot), published three years earlier. Burroughs would revisit Hollywood and film-making to good effect later with his 1934 novel *Tarzan and the Lion Man*, which features some highly amusing movie-related passages.

And, by the time *Tarzan and the Lion Man* hit bookstores, Hollywood, and a new breed of sleuth dubbed the Hollywood detective, had found their way into the pulp magazines.

Throughout my career as a writer and researcher, I've found that calling *anything* the first of its kind is a little like being the fastest gun in the West; there's always someone out there ready and willing to challenge you—and maybe win. So I'm not going to venture a guess as to when the Hollywood detective first took hold in the pulps. I can say, though, that one of the first of any consequence was Perley Poore Sheehan's Doctor Coffin, the Living Dead Man, whose adventures appeared in the *Thrilling Mystery* pulp during 1932 and '33. (Several of those tales were collected, with an introduction by yours truly, in a 2007 book from Off-Trail Press.) Doctor Coffin is a Tinseltown undertaker who's actually Del Manning, the movies' "Man of 500 Faces" (an obvious knockoff of silent-picture star Lon Chaney's nickname, "the Man of 1,000 Faces") whom everyone thinks is dead.

If Doctor Coffin's crime-fighting persona is a little convoluted, Dan Turner's is just about as simple and straightforward as you can get. Debuting in the June 1934 issue of *Spicy Detective Stories*, Robert Leslie Bellem's *uber*-breezy creation fought, drank, shot, wisecracked and, well, *loved* his way through some 300 tales written for a number of different pulp titles, including the long-running *Hollywood Detective*, published regularly for over eight years. Much has been written about Dan, by others as well as myself, over the years, and there are any number of Turner collections available (including my own, Adventure House's 2003 book *Roscoes in the Night*, and Bowling Green State University Popular Press' Robert Leslie Bellem's *Dan Turner, Hollywood Detective* [1983], the first book of Dan's stories to see print). The character was so popular that Bellem created a number of other Hollywood dicks, including the stuntman Nick Ransom, who showed up in *Thrilling Detective* at just about the time the studio system began to crumble.

Still another noteworthy Tinseltown sleuth was created by Bellem's pal and sometime collaborator, W.T. Ballard. Ballard's Bill Lennox, a "troubleshooter" for General Consolidated

Studios, appeared in the famed *Black Mask* magazine for about a decade, from 1933 into 1942, before spinning off into novels.

And then we come to Tony Key, "the World's Highest Paid Detective," whose adventures are collected for the first time in this volume. An ex-G-man, he's ostensibly a big-time Hollywood agent. Actually, he's employed by a cabal of top Tinseltown producers to function as a crime-solver whenever the lid blows off something involving them or their studios. While his allegedly confidential identity as a detective seems to become less and less of a secret as time goes by, his supporting cast gets more and more interesting as the stories progress. So do the one-shot players, who often show up in lengthy sequences before Key is even introduced.

Of course, where can you find better characters than in Golden Age Hollywood?

That includes their real-life creator, the prolific Steve Fisher—who, for the better part of his life, would not only write fiction set in that city, but would also make it his home.

WHILE SEVERAL SOURCES list Steven Gould Fisher's mother as an actress, I've been unable to ascertain whether or not she had any movie credits. We do know that she and her son lived in Southern California, beginning somewhere around the early '20s. During that time, the Hollywood area offered all sorts of show-biz opportunities beyond movies; Los Angeles was known as a center of the vaudeville circuit then, so it's possible Mrs. Fisher was employed by that once-thriving form of popular entertainment. It could also have been that she was touring with a legitimate-theater company. In an unbylined editorial called "The Hard Way" in the June 1941 issue of *Detective Tales,* the author—likely Rogers Terrill— wrote, "[B]ecause she traveled with road companies for weeks on end, he [Fisher] was a lonesome little cuss farmed out to various relatives during his formative years."

A 2019 entry on the *Age of Aces* website (ageofaces.net) notes that because of her frequent road trips, she ultimately enrolled her son at a school called Oneonta Military Academy. There's no mention in any biographies I've seen of his father, so it may be that his mother was separated or a divorcee. What's clear is that she'd traveled with her son from Marine City, Michigan, where he was born (on August 29, 1912) to California, finally packing him off to Oneonta, which boasted a 22-acre campus in the L.A. suburb of South Pasadena—about a dozen miles from Hollywood.

So, it's not exactly correct to say that Steve Fisher moved to Southern California when he began selling his work to the movie studios; it was, in fact, a return to his roots.

But as a teen, he couldn't wait to get out of the place. In fact, according to the *Age of Aces* entry, he hated life at Oneonta so much that he ran away at the age of 16 and enlisted in the Navy, leaving military school for the real military. The June '41 *Detective Tales* piece puts a more romantic spin on his getaway: "Steve joined the Navy when a Spanish girl with whom he fell desperately in love, ditched him for another guy. He served on battleships and submarines, and at last the story-a-week sched-ule he had kept up for years began to bear fruit."

This would've been around 1928. By that time, according to the *Detective Tales* narrative, young Steve had been writing stories regularly for 16 years—beginning at the age of six.

In a 2017 piece on the blackmaskmagazine.com website,

Keith Alan Deutsch wrote that Fisher spent some of his active-duty time in Honolulu; he would employ the islands, along with the Navy, as settings throughout his writing career. Indeed, even when his milieu was as far away from Hawaii as Hollywood, Fisher would often find a way to incorporate the South Seas into a story—as can be seen in several of the tales collected here.

While still a teenaged seaman, he began selling fiction and nonfiction to service-connected publications like *U.S. Navy* and *Our Navy*. Wrote Deutsch, "After he was discharged from service in Los Angeles in 1932, Fisher stayed in L.A. and continued to write for *U.S. Navy* at a penny a word." (In his memoir, *The Pulp Jungle* [Sherbourne Press, 1967], Fisher's longtime pal and fellow pulp scribe Frank Gruber recalled that U.S. Navy paid Fisher "something like a tenth of a cent a word.") Fisher also saw some success with the girlie-mag market, selling hotcha shorts to the likes of *Paris Nights, Love Revels,* and *Zippy* over the next couple of years.

In 1934, he moved to New York City, the epicenter of the pulps, and while he managed to eke out a few sales, he found it tough sledding. Once again, from the *Detective Tales* piece: "He ate boiled potatoes for weeks; wore his shoe leather thin, wrote in a cold, bare attic apartment in Greenwich Village— while the wolf and the landlord grimly circled in for the kill."

Added Frank Gruber, in *The Pulp Jungle:*

> Those first few months in New York were bitterly cruel on Steve. He could not catch on. He was evicted from his first Greenwich Village apartment, then got three month's credit in a five-story walkup. The manager was a former Navy man and for that

reason decided to give Steve the credit. The apartment was virtually unrentable, anyway.

One afternoon I climbed the stairs and found Steve writing a letter to the electric company. He let me read it. It was an impassioned plea not to turn off his electricity. How would the electric light company feel, Steve asked, if they had turned off the electricity on Jack London? Well, he was going to be as big a success one day and the electric light company would be ashamed of itself.

The cold-hearted electric light company did not give a damn about Jack London, or Steve. The next time I went to see Steve he had only candlelight.

Steve was evicted from his second apartment the day before Christmas of 1934. With a typewriter under one arm, a suitcase under the other, he trudged the streets, block by block. He finally found a landlord who was willing to take a chance on him without a down payment on the rent.

The good news for Fisher was that, by Christmas of the following year, he'd placed some three dozen stories with various pulp publishers, including the giants Street & Smith (which began running tales of his Naval Intelligence officer Sheridan Doome, whose body and face had been hideously rearranged by an explosion, in the pages of the hugely popular hero pulp *The Shadow*) and Popular Publications, notably in *The Mysterious Wu Fang*, a short-lived Fu Manchu knock-off responsible for introducing him to his future wife, Edythe Seims, who was editing the book for Popular at the time.

According to the *Detective Tale*s piece, he'd gotten the *Wu Fang* gig because Seims found herself needing "an Oriental story" for the back of the book. "Steve had been to the Orient, so he wrote a story and took it to Miss Seims. And promptly fell in love. Several weeks later, he stole one of our best editors by marrying Edythe Seims."

That would've been in 1935, a breakthrough year for Fisher and his work. The floodgates opened and his prose flowed through, inundating the pulps, eventually filtering into the slick magazines, and, ultimately, the movies. He penned some fine novels along the way, including the harrowing Hollywood-set *I Wake up Screaming* (1941, made into a first-class A-film and released on Halloween of the same year by 20th Century-Fox) and *The Big Dream* (1970), one of his final books, which offers an insightful insider's look at the tensions existing then between theatrical filmmakers and TV people. (Fisher's final scripts were for the television series *Starsky & Hutch, Switch,* and *Fantasy Island;* he died in 1980, six years after his wife.)

By the time *The Big Dream* came out, Fisher had been living in Hollywood for some 30 years, with both an Academy Award nomination (for scripting 1944's *Destination Tokyo*) and a Writers Guild of America Award nomination (for a 1960 episode of TV's *Jane Wyman Presents the Fireside Theatre*) to his credit.

But as noteworthy as his work in TV and the movies was, his contributions to pulp literature deserve at least equal consideration. He was, in fact, a pulp-magazine innovator, one of a wave of writers who changed the very style of pulp-detective fiction. Another Keith Alan Deutsch posting, this one from 2012 on the website somethingisgoingtohappen.net, called it "The Ellsworth Shift," after the *Black Mask* editor Fanny Ellsworth, who had taken over the helm of the influential detective pulp from Joseph T. Shaw in 1936. To Deutsch, under Ellsworth the prose in the magazine then began shifting "from the objective, hardboiled writing promoted by Shaw and the earlier editors of *Black Mask* magazine to the subjective, psychologically and emotionally heightened writing that came in vogue under her guidance."

Fisher himself, in a January 1972 *Armchair Detective* piece, described it as "the subculture revolution in the pulps during the late 1930s—which, translated, means how styles changed, one school, objective writing, let's call it 'hardboiled,' phasing out, and subjective, 'tough'—which is better described as 'tough-tender,' replacing it."

Using his friend Roger Torrey, as well as Dashiell Hammett, as examples of the old-school style, he added that they "wrote objectively, with crisp, cold precision, no emotion was described. You saw what happened from the outside but were never permitted inside a fictional character."

Like Deutsch, he believed all that changed when Ellsworth took the helm of *Black Mask* and he and his friends Frank Gruber and Cornell Woolrich, among others, began selling stories to her that were characterized by a "subjective style and mood."

"Personalization" is, I think, another way to describe that approach. You can see it in every one of the tales in this volume. Often, Tony Key doesn't even show up for several pages; instead, Fisher puts us in the shoes of someone else—sometimes a person who won't even make it to the end of the story. He personalizes his characters in a way that was, indeed, pretty revolutionary for that time and place. Even though only one of these tales originally appeared in Ellsworth's *Black Mask*—

the rest seeing print in a rival publication, *Detective Fiction Weekly*—what Fisher described in his *Armchair Detective* essay is right at the heart of each Tony Key adventure, and easy to spot.

These yarns are driven by the characters, and Fisher gives us some memorable ones here. There aren't, for instance, many hotter female sidekicks in the pulps than Betty Gale, Key's fiancée and fellow adventurer, who gives off a snappy Jean Harlow vibe. Other recurring players—from the nosy Western Union delivery boy Sonny Lloyd to the oleaginous thug Tip Martin—are fine and believable creations as well.

Although Steve Fisher wouldn't settle in Southern California for good until a half-decade or so after these stories were written, his understanding of the place and his facility for crafting characters who might really have lived in Golden Age Hollywood shine through every page. The Tony Key stories may have indeed been in the vanguard of a revolution in pulp writing, but you don't have to know that to enjoy them.

—John Wooley
Foyil, Oklahoma
11 April 2024

(Once again, my thanks to Matt Moring for the opportunity and to John Locke, my pulp-research hero.)

Death On Set 13

*Tony Key, The World's Highest Paid Detective,
Was Forced to Earn His Salary, When That
Movie Murder Blew the Lid Off Hollywood*

1

HE HAD FINISHED a pint of whisky, but he was sober; sober now, suddenly, when a moment before his mind had been fogged, and the fume of the liquor had been on his breath. The thin, fine specks of sweat oozed through his tan grease paint. His face was glistening brown; the eyes bloodshot, yet sharp, little flames burning in them; the loose mouth now in a grim and even line.

He was sober, and he watched the kid put down his cards and reach over and scoop his last ten dollars into his lap. Jack Swanson's voice was flat, he said:

"You are lucky, Brandon."

Brandon was a chorus boy, fresh out of a Los Angeles college, and he grinned weakly; but there was no humor in it; nor any humor in the faces around the little table.

"Yeah," Brandon said, "I guess I am."

Everyone was looking at Jack Swanson, and the silence was tense and heavy so that he felt it. Everyone was waiting for him—good old Jack whose career had been a long if not glorious one through horse opera to playing a Park Avenue gentleman; and who at fifty, long, lean and gray-haired, was still trying to be cast as a dashing juvenile—to put down his cards and say he was through.

The sound stage was quiet, even back here in the darkest corner where no one spoke. Behind Swanson, a long way behind, it seemed, flood lights gradually reached out shafts of whiteness. Something snapped, like a cracker. A voice called for silence, and another voice: "Camera—Action."

"Don't move," snapped Tony, "you're covered!"

Jack Swanson should have put down his cards to say that he was going over and watch the scene, but he couldn't. He was trembling, and so cold sober that he could feel his heart hammering against his side. He had worked only six days, but each day he had played—telling Ann they were going to pay him by the week, instead of by the day, as they were paying him—and each day he had lost.

Six hundred badly needed dollars. The picture needed him in only one more shot, so after today he would be finished. He knew, thought he knew, what Ann would say when he came home with only one day's pay envelope.

This work in *Pride of the Nation* had been his first in over a year, and when Central Casting had called him, he remem-

bered Ann, face lined, peroxided hair with streaks of gray in it; stringy, because she had not had a permanent for months. How bright her eyes had been, how deeply thankful her voice.

"I don't care what you say about Sam Schmidt," she had said, "he is good, and kind. After what we did to him—it would take most men more than ten years to get over it. He's given you this part because he knows we need money, *I* need money. There's something awful decent about that, don't you think?"

"Decent?" Jack Swanson had replied, "don't be silly, Ann. He's still the shrewd producer he was when he coined two million for himself. *Pride of the Nation* is to be a big thing, containing a galaxy. I'm a star, and he knows he can get me cheap. Imagine, a hundred a day—"

"He might have had you cheaper," she reminded him.

"Who said so? Cranston, that agent? What does he know? I'm quits with him. Quits with all agents!"

"Just the same," Ann said softly, "I think he's nice. Seven

hundred dollars will save us from—let's not say what from. Let us just say that it will save us. To do that for me, a faithless wife who deserted him for a handsome actor. Well, it brings home to me that there is something in Hollywood except tinsel."

"I tell you his motive is purely commercial," Jack had snapped angrily. "He swore he'd make me sorry someday for taking you, and he hasn't forgotten so quickly. He has some other reason."

And now, he sat there, staring at the paste-board cards which lay unshuffled on the table. He was conscious of the embarrassed silence, the eyes of the others. Particularly two of the men who stared at him now, and in whose hearts, as well as his own, lay a deep rooted and mutual hatred.

In Hollywood you drank and laughed and gambled with your enemies sometimes; and suffered the jealousy of their success, and smugly swelled when you did something better than they. It was life: a kind of a game in which the winner took all, and the loser ranted bitterly of injustice to talent.

JACK SWANSON BROUGHT a piece of paper from his pocket, fished nervously over his clothing for a pencil. He was sweating too much, breathing too hard. He scribbled awkwardly across the paper:

IOU
One Hundred Dollars
Payable this date at the cashier's booth.

He shoved it to the center of the table, and looked up at Percy Brandon. "Do you mind risking your—winnings, against that?"

The chorus boy's eyes were hot. His face was in the shadow,

but Jack could see the glint in his blue eyes, the smooth shine on his blond hair; the weak jaw. Brandon wet his lips.

"Listen, old man," he said, "I—"

"Put up your hundred," Jack said coldly. "And if I ever find out that you've been cheating during these games—I am not saying that you have. Men *do* have uncanny luck, but—" He clipped the sentence there, the flames in his eyes burning brighter. Brandon shrugged helplessly and shoved five twenties out on the table.

Jack looked at the next man, who, too, had won no small portion in the games of chance.

"You, Chesterton? Straight draw for the pot. No ante, no bidding."

Luke Chesterton was a round-faced little man who wore horn-rimmed glasses, taking them off only when he was acting. He had come from Broadway, where they called him funny, to be part of the galaxy in *Pride of the Nation.* He was one of the men who hated Jack Swanson, and his resigned expression indicated that he was disgusted that things had turned out as dramatically as they had. Although he commanded a high salary, he was a frugal man, and when he had come into the game it was ten-cent ante.

He pushed ten ten-dollar bills out into the table and spoke in a low-toned voice. "This isn't fair, Swanson. We are not debted to you to give you a chance of gaining back what you have lost. I am doing it only because it gives me great pleasure to fill the begging hand of the man who, five years ago, was such a big handsome hero at a certain party in Malibu." Bright eyes shone from beneath the panes of his glasses.

Jack knew what he meant. It had been another time when

Luke Chesterton was working in Hollywood and he was head over heels in love with Myrna Bow, who had since made a good marriage. Jack Swanson had been intoxicated, and when an opportunity had arisen to ridicule the dumpy little Broadway comedian, he had been merciless. Until work on *Pride of the Nation* had begun last week, he had not seen Chesterton since, and it was with surprise that he had learned the comedian still nursed the bitter grudge against him.

Bill Borden, extra and bit player who had never tasted real fame in all his long life, and who had once tried to blackmail Jack, was the next man. His daily pay was only twenty-five dollars and he had a desperate need for the money. Thin, sallow face bitter, he shook his head as Jack looked toward him.

"You can count me out."

But as he stared into Jack Swanson's eyes a change suddenly came over Bill Borden; it was as if he had looked into the face of death. Reluctantly, not knowing himself why he did it, he pushed a great stack of five, ten and one dollar bills into the pot, and came into the game.

Jack Swanson picked up the deck. He gazed at Percy Brandon; at Luke Chesterton; at Bill Borden. The other man at the table had neither won nor lost and could not be asked to risk a hundred dollars.

Jack shuffled, his fingers cold and tingling as he sifted the heavy cards. Silently, he began to deal. When he was through he picked up his cards. A drum seemed to beat wildly in his mind. Two aces! Quickly, he discarded three, glanced around. Brandon took only one, Chesterton two, and Bill Borden, his wrinkled face creased in an expression of hatred, four.

JACK SWANSON SQUEEZED the cards now, looked at them. Bill Borden threw down his hand and got up and left the table. Chesterton laid down a pair of nines. Shaking, laughter bubbling from his soul, Jack put down three aces. Eyes hot, feverish and hot, he looked toward Percy Brandon.

The youth laid down four deuces.

For a moment Jack Swanson could not breathe, could not think. He felt as though cold water were drenching his face, his body, and leaving him shivering. He laughed, although it was more like a hoarse cackle, and it rasped his throat, and then he pushed back the table and got to his feet.

He walked, knowing no sense of direction, nor reason; feeling numb in mind and in muscles, and drunk again suddenly, so that he reeled. He heard music coming from the splendid inside set that was now shooting. *Aloha Oe…* Farewell… Farewell.

He left the set, went outside, and walked through the dirt of the street, past the big sound stages, past the cottages; and the music did not leave his ears, but played over and over again, making him remember his first picture when he had played as a subordinate to Tom Mix. And then the others, through the years, where he had been a fast riding, hard-shooting hero; or a fast talking, romantic hero.

Suddenly he realized he was walking down the board walk in front of the studio's executive offices. He was in front of the office of the president. Frosted glass door, and gold letters: *"Samuel Schmidt—Executive Producer."*

He said hoarsely: "Sam will loan me some. He has to. Sam with millions. He still loves Ann. He'll loan me the money. I'm not through yet. Not by a long way."

He did not knock. He put his hand on the cold bronze knob of the door and turned it.

He entered the office. Sam Schmidt looked from his desk, and the cigar that was in his mouth went limp.

Jack Swanson closed the door as though it required great effort to close it. He leaned back, and a half smile, half stupor fanned weakly over his lined face.

"I came to see you, Sam," he said. "First time in ten years. I want to talk to you. You don't mind talking to anybody so measly as an actor, do you? You aren't so busy that the guy who took your wife can't get a word in, are you? I hope not, because there are some things I want to say, see? Some things I've been wanting to say for a long time."

2

Tony Key

ON THE DOOR of a Hollywood Boulevard office was the proclamation:

ANTHONY KEY

Exclusive Representative

Motion Pictures

However, unlike the office doors of movie agents, this one was never locked. And if you were a bit player whose weary business it was to pack a Sunday smile and a big bluff into a brief case and drag it around with you from casting office to casting office, and agent to agent—if you were this, or a faded star, or a writer whose option was up in a week, or any one of the other human beings desperate enough to chance any door that had the mark of "agency" on it, and you entered Anthony Key's office, you would not be surprised at what you saw, unless it happened that you were impressed with lavishness.

You would wade through a thick black rug into which your heels would sink until they were out of sight. You might sit on one of the expensive plush leather chairs and wait your turn, or, if the place were empty, go directly to the girl who sat at the shiny black ebony desk, and who wore a patent leather dress that fitted tightly about her hips, and matched, curiously enough, the ebony. You would say: "I am Herman Horowitz. DeMille once told me—"

And she, the lovely girl, her platinum hair a radiant halo against the ominous black; her face warm, the glistening red of her lips curved in a slight and heartening smile, would tell you that Mr. Key was not at liberty, at present, to take on additional talent.

Which was true, for as a matter-of-fact, Anthony Key was not, is not, an agent. Of course you didn't know that. But the Hays office knows it; so does the Los Angeles Police, and the Department of Justice. However, combined with only a handful of the biggest producers and studio executives, they are all who share the secret.

Anthony Key, whose salary was one of the biggest in Hollywood, was known to the general public only as a more or less "minor" agent.

Anthony Key was, is, the world's highest paid detective.

The voice that came through the wire was high, shrill, and very excited. As Tony Key listened to it, he was conscious of a queer feeling surging up through his stomach and into his chest. There had been robbery, and fraud, and blackmailing, but not for a long time had there been murder.

And if he were going to squash all publicity, and get the papers to list Jack Swanson's death as "natural" and save, as Schmidt said, a three hundred thousand dollar production from ruin, he would have to hustle.

He said: "Okay, Mr. Schmidt."

Five minutes later, still on the phone, he said: "Okay, Mr. Schmidt."

Ten minutes later he said it again, and hung up. He swung about in the swivel chair, drew a pad of paper toward him and began writing. His hair was black, smoothly combed; his face was so tan he looked like an actor made-up; the white of his teeth, and the green of his eyes, made contrast. He was young.

A year or so ago he had been a Federal Agent.

THERE WAS A reason why he got it, of course. He had cracked a half a dozen studio cases, as a G man; and he had chalked up scores in deduction that were almost unbelievable. He could shoot, and fly, and ride horse back; and he handled his fists like Gene Tunney.

He wore a neat blue suit, a white sweater; and a hidden shoulder holster in which nestled a slim blue automatic. He rang the bell on his desk now, and looked up at the platinum blond as she entered.

"We've a murder in our lap, Betty."

Her eyebrows lifted. "That's a break."

He said quietly: "Jack Swanson."

"Hmm. A biggie who's been laying eggs lately. Where was he working?"

"Paramet," Tony answered, and he leaned back and caught his breath; lit a cigarette. Just looking at Betty Gale gave him a throbbing pulse. She had been a stock girl at one of the studios when he "rescued" her; and he was still afraid to let her go near a studio for fear somebody might decide to make her a star. It was his fond idea that if he were persistent enough, he could, eventually, make her Mrs. Key.

"Paramet," she repeated, then snapped her fingers. "Oh, that supergigantic colossal pic where everybody in the cast is supposed to be a star. It'll sort of freeze the box office, if we don't turn on the hush-hush, won't it?"

"It might also very well freeze our jobs," Tony said. "Gather the cast." The "cast" was Tony Key's staff of talent who, the moment a crime occurred, drifted unobtrusively onto the scene, forming his own private spy net.

"Oke," said Betty, and went to the door. She turned. "How about me, too? Daisy will take the office, if—"

He slapped his hand on the desk. "Absolutely not! You stay *here!* On the phone. There may be—"

But she had slammed the door after her.

Twenty-two minutes later Tony Key was in Schmidt's private office where the corpse lay on its side, a knife—hilt deep—in the back.

Jack Swanson's face seemed to be frozen stiff, rigid. His eyes, like pieces of glass, were staring straight ahead. He clutched, half-clutched, in his hand, a little bronze lion paper weight. Tony looked up, his green eyes flickering.

"Why did you kill him, Mr. Schmidt?"

Sam Schmidt's fat, flabby face, was dripping with sweat; half a cigar, unlighted, ragged, bobbed up and down in his mouth as he spoke. His small brown eyes glowed like livid spots of varnish.

"For the love of Pete, you don't think I did it? Think *I* would call you over here if I had did a thing like that? You must be mad. *I've* been going crazy waiting for you to get here! I'm nervous; I'm going to pieces! All this time I have been here with him, *that*—" he looked at the corpse, "alone with him, his eyes looking at me, his lips sneering. Dead lips sneering; dead eyes looking—"

"I know," Tony said quietly, "you told me that on the phone." He glanced at an open window, walked over and examined it. "This isn't usually open, is it? In fact, until now, it hasn't been opened since it was last painted; because chips of the paint fell off when you forced it to open. You told me over the phone that while your back was turned you heard Swanson call out. You looked around, saw a figure vanish past the window. Then you noticed there was a knife in Swanson's back."

"Yes, that's right. That's exactly what happened."

"What was the occasion then, for opening the window?"

"While you're about it, you might tell me *why* you didn't pull the knife out of Swanson?"

SCHMIDT TOOK THE cigar from his mouth. "You're on the wrong track," he barked. "Why should I want to kill that ham and egger? The window was open because he came in here threatening me and I opened it so that in the case he became violent I could call out. As for the knife, to pull it out would have caused a profusion of blood. And he was dead before he hit the floor."

"You are *sure* of that?"

"Well, I—I thought I was."

Tony Key grinned, a tight grin that told nothing of what he thought; yet was affable. "Okay, Mr. Schmidt. But you have to admit that the cops would hit you harder than that under the circumstances. You're on a pretty tough spot."

"I know—oh I know it all right. That's what I get for trying to be nice to him."

He picked up a new cigar, bit off the end, and nervously lit it.

Tony looked around, glanced back at the corpse, then up at the producer. "Keep them working. All night if you have to. Tell them there's orders to make it a rush job. And remember, not a word about *this*—" he jerked his thumb in the direction of Swanson.

"Don't worry," Sam Schmidt assured him, "I—" The phone clattered shrilly, and he picked it up, looking nervously at Tony. "Yes? *What?* I see— Oh! All right, I'll see her." He hung up, his voice was tense. "It was sound stage six where *Pride of the Nation* is shooting. Britton, my director said a crazy woman has been running around there. She's headed for my office now—"

"—But she is not crazy," a voice from the window said.

Tony Key saw what he thought was an old woman. Her face might have been pretty, but there were lines in it, and red streaks where tears had washed off the powder. There were black pockets under her burning eyes; and her thick blonde-gray hair was a disarrayed mat.

"Ann," Schmidt gasped, "Ann Swanson!"

She said hoarsely: "Yes, Ann Swanson. I am looking for the man I love, and the man you hate. What have you done with him? Oh, I know you've done something. That it was you who wrote this note. I should have seen through it when you hired him, but I—"

She broke off suddenly; in the next second a high, shrill scream broke from her lips.

3

The Man in the Mask

A FEW MINUTES later they pulled her, still sobbing, from the corpse of her husband and forced her to sit down in the big leather chair. She was still hysterically accusing Schmidt of the murder, but Tony Key managed to get her to give him the note she had received. While she sat moaning, rocking back and forth, he took it back to the desk and read it.

> *To Ann Swanson:*
>
> *You and your husband are going to die.*
>
> *You know the reason.*
>
> *I am telling you in advance so you may know, and suffer in the knowledge.*

It was printed, and unsigned.

"When did you receive this?"

"A few minutes ago," she answered, wiping her tear-stained face. "We live only down the street, and naturally I hurried right to the studio to see Jack."

Tony Key's smooth face was without expression, and his green eyes were hard. "It says you know the reason. What is it?"

Eyes hot, she looked at Schmidt. "He knows. He can tell you."

For a moment Tony Key did not move. He glanced at Schmidt, back at Ann Swanson. Then he got up and closed the window, bolting it. He turned the lock in the door, and went back to the phone, he put his hand on it, but before picking it up, said:

"So far as I am concerned, this case starts right now. Schmidt, you and Mrs. Swanson are going to remain in this office. Under guard. Both for your protection, and to prevent either of you from escaping. I suspect you both. If I have made myself clear on that point, I will proceed."

"By all means do," Schmidt breathed.

"All right, if neither of you are the killer, the killer is not aware of how fatal was his knife; even though he may well suspect that he has successfully killed Jack Swanson. But it would have been improbable for him to linger long enough to make sure. Therefore, it is reasonable to believe that if the murderer sees Swanson alive, realizes that he has only wounded him, he will make another attempt to bring about his death as quickly as possible. Do you both agree?"

Ann Swanson said in a heavy whisper: "You are a young fool who is wasting his time. Sam Schmidt is responsible for what has happened!"

"In that case," Tony Key went on, "there will be no attempt made on Jack Swanson's life, and I will know—"

Schmidt leapt to his feet. "What are you talking about? Swanson is dead! He can't return to life! Have *you* gone crazy, or have I?"

Tony Key leaned across the desk, spoke slowly. "I cannot vouch for you, Mr. Schmidt. As for myself, I deem it advisable to assume the role of Jack Swanson. In a few minutes my makeup expert, and a man who will be armed to *protect* you and Mrs. Swanson while you remain here in the office, will be here. In a very few minutes, if Betty Gale has not fallen down on me."

He lifted the phone now, called his own office. His eyes were cold, hard, and his lips were tight; but when Betty came on the phone, without changing expression, his voice became suddenly smooth.

"Hello, Sugar. This is Papa who is already up to his neck, and doing nicely, thank you. Listen. I want you to send Curley and Max down here right away. Mr. Schmidt's office. They are to speak to no one—just use their passes. Tell Max to bring his bag of tricks along. I am going to represent a corpse who got up and walked again. Mr. Schmidt told me when he called, how Swanson had been playing cards. Well—"

TONY KEY CAME in through the sliding door, and walked straight out to the edge of the South Sea shack set which was numbered "13." He uncorked a bottle of whisky, and leaning against the scenery, gulped some down. He wiped his mouth with the back of his hand and jammed the bottle back into his pocket. He blinked now because the slow, powerful klieg lamps were beginning to come back on. The huge camera, cords extending from it to the sound machine, slid down its tracks for a close up. The first cameraman adjusted the big square "eye" and stand-ins for the stars stood in while the second cameraman posed them first one way, then another.

The skinny, second-assistant director was rushing about screaming for the carpenter to bring in a few more buckets of sand for Waikiki Beach; and presently the sun—the biggest and most costly lamp of all—began to come on, and even at thirty feet, almost scorched the grass roof of the hut. Myrna

Bow, rich red hair streaming down her shoulders as far as the shapely thighs which were adorned with a grass skirt, stood watching from one of the wings.

Presently the actors came in and took the place of the stand-ins. Britton, the heavy-set director, came forward.

He looked very grim and pompous; wore a white turtle-neck sweater. The script in his hand, he said: "You, Miss Bow. A moment after I have called action. You look to where Harry will enter, saying: 'But you can not go, my darling. You must not go. I am white, but I have adopted these people; and you must adopt them, too.' Say that now, please."

She said it, and Britton faded back even with the camera. The lights were getting brighter each moment. Suddenly the distant slopes of Diamond Head began to tremble.

Britton looked around and his face went white: *"Mr. Swanson,"* he shrieked. "You are leaning on the scenery! Will you *please, please* get the hell out of the way!"

Tony Key moved quickly away from the scenery, grumbling to himself. Luckily, Britton had shouted loud enough to have his voice heard all over the sound stage, and Tony figured that about now a killer's heart should be up in his mouth; provided, of course, that the killer was here.

He moved back through the scenery that was not in use, back farther into the shadows where various cliques of extras, bit players, and stars who were not needed for the present shot were resting, playing bridge, or poker, or talking in whispers. Deep into the right, rear corner he came upon the flimsy table on which Swanson had lost six hundred dollars and an IOU chit. Six men were sitting about it, deeply intent in a game of poker.

This was Hollywood, Tony Key thought. They paid you for a day's work; paid the actors and extras, and whenever they actually had to get up and go on the set for a shot, they grumbled until they were allowed to retire to the wings again.

It was a great life. They would starve one day, and grumble during work at the next.

BUT THERE WERE things more important than summarizing the character defects of filmdom's lesser entities: Percy Brandon's hat was stuffed with money, and the blond chorus boy was wearing a grim, almost mocking smile. Luke Chesterton's eyes were almost popping from beneath the horn-rimmed glasses. The comedian from Broadway had ripped off his tie, and he was sweating profusely. It was apparent that he had been losing. Bill Borden, a stack of five dollar bills in front of him, looked uneasy, unsatisfied; it appeared that the old bit player was just breaking even.

There were others at the table, of course, but these were the men Tony Key had gained the information about while Max made a wax—pliable-mould of Jack Swanson's dead face, for him; while his hair was dyed, and grease paint was splashed over him. He even wore the clothes Swanson had been wearing, including the knife-gash and blood on the back of the coat.

The three were so intent on their game that they had not noticed him. "Mind if I get in?" Tony asked in a flat voice.

The three men looked up as one. The smug smile dropped from Percy Brandon's face. He brought out a handkerchief, wiped his forehead, cast a glance at the others. Bill Borden, lighting a cigarette, grunted: "Sure, but no more four hundred dollar pots." Luke Chesterton was trembling, and silent.

One of the extras got up and Tony Key sat down. It was just light enough to see the cards and he knew no one would penetrate the disguise. He flipped a hundred dollar note across the table.

"My I O U, Brandon."

Brandon laughed nervously and tore it up. He put the bill in his hat.

Bill Borden leaned forward. "Where did you get the cash?"

"Friend of mine," Tony Key said evenly. "He wasn't going to do it, but somebody tried to knife me. He wasn't a very good shot. By the way, where did you boys go after I left the table?"

"*I* didn't go anywhere," Bill Borden said hotly. "Percy and Chesterton were called for a shot. Why? You don't think we tried to knife you, do you?"

Tony Key laughed, shook his head. He passed the bottle around, then took a nip himself. At last he threw two tens and a five into the center of the table. "I'm for a twenty-five dollar ante. Make things interesting."

Two of the men at the table immediately withdrew, but Brandon, Chesterton and Borden contributed silently, and one of the other men, a dapper little extra, fished the amount out of his pocket to be dealt in.

Tony Key picked up the cards, and he was conscious that they felt heavy in his hands. His eyes were on the players; sharply watching each one of them. Quietly, he dealt, picking up only a pair of fives.

After the discard he picked up another five.

When everyone laid down Chesterton had three tens; Perry Brandon, grinning again now, three jacks.

"I win," Tony Key said quietly. He looked across the table. "And I'll take exactly seven hundred and twenty-five dollars."

4

Death Comes Again

SWEAT RAN, STREAKED, across Percy Brandon's face, and his blue eyes were hot. For a moment he was unable to move, and then he tried to laugh. But his eyes were directed down at the table where Tony Key's finger pried a card apart, so that it made two separate cards. That was why the deck had felt heavy.

If you knew the trick you could double everything you had, making a pair into four of a kind; and later, in the shuffle, slide the cards together again, dissolving four into two again.

"You play a nice game, Brandon," Tony said softly.

The blond chorus boy shoved his chair back a little; his eyes had not left Tony's. Chesterton was staring at Brandon; Bill Borden stared also. At last Brandon spoke, in a whisper.

"Don't get sore, guys," he pleaded. "I'll give you the dough, all of it, my own included. It was just that I was desperate. I wanted to get away from Hollywood. Go somewhere and live a quiet, decent life. I—" he choked, "I thought you knew, Swanson, I—"

"Is that why you threw a knife at me?"

"No! I swear I didn't do that." Brandon got to his feet clutching the hat full of money. His face was drained white and Tony could see the throbbing in his temples. The kid dumped the hat on the table. "There take it, all of it, and—"

A scream, the high, shrill scream of a woman echoed and

reechoed suddenly through the sound stage. Following the first cry there were more screams, other screams. A babble of voices rising into a furious din.

Tony Key leapt from the chair, raced through the scenery to set number 13. A crowd of people were surrounding a figure who lay prone in the sand. Tony barged through quickly. He saw the beautiful star Myrna Bow lying on her back, eyes closed. Britton was rubbing her wrists.

"Get Mr. Schmidt," he commanded.

Both of the assistant directors took up the call and it was echoed by the script girl. Tony bent down beside the director.

"What's the matter?"

Britton glanced around at him. "Get out of here, Swanson. She's dead. You can see that, can't you?"

"Dead, but I—"

"Get back, Swanson. Get back!"

Tony Key felt the star's pulse. It had stopped, all right, though there were no marks of physical violence on her body. He got up, pushed out through the crowd, and left the sound stage through the sliding doors. It was getting dark.

He met Schmidt rushing toward the stage in tow of Curley—a squat, heavyset man whose hair was a mop of black ringlets, and whose nose was squashed back in his face.

"Schmidt said he had to come down here, boss," were his first words.

"He does," Tony Key snapped. "You'll find Doc White inside. Get him to pronounce Myrna Bow's death due to heart failure."

Sam Schmidt whirled about, his flabby face white. "Then she *is* dead?"

"I'm afraid so."

"Oh my God!"

Curley Conley looked grim. "I don't see how we're going to keep the cops away now, boss."

"Nor do I," Tony Key snapped, "but we've got a head start, and we have to crack this case damn soon, before anything else can happen. I'm going to Miss Bow's dressing room. She looks as though she has been poisoned. Bring Britton over as soon as you can get hold of him."

"Okay, what about Schmidt?"

"You'll have to let him do what he wants. This thing has grown too big for the procedure we had mapped out."

TONY RUSHED AWAY, back behind the sound stage, and down the aisle off which were dressing room doors. Myrna Bow rated a cottage on the lot, but she was using one of the smaller dressing rooms for quick changes. He came to the one with her name on the door and went inside.

Tony Key did not know what his thoughts were, he knew only that they were not coherent thoughts, and that whatever scheme he had carefully wrapped in his kit to solve a case in a cut and dried way, had now to be discarded. He had picked up two or three clues, but at best, he was still in the dark, and he could only move forward in the grim way of a crime solving machine.

He glanced about the dressing room, saw the clothes, the make-up box. Suddenly he stooped, picked up a candy wrapper. He examined it carefully, then looked around for the candy. It was gone, had probably been eaten by the star.

"What—what do you want here?" a hoarse voice behind him asked.

He spun about to see a colored maid. She stepped into the dressing room but sagged back against the door suddenly; her eyes rolled until they showed white and hideous.

"Your—your stomach?" Tony asked.

Already she was sliding off her feet. He took her into his arms and laid her down gently. He could see traces of chocolate on her lips, around the corners of her dusky mouth; particles of the poison candy that had clung. It was evidently a poison that did not work until a few minutes after it was taken.

He left her to grab the phone and call for a doctor, but he saw as he picked up the instrument, that she was dead. If nothing else, the poison struck hard once it got working. There could be no mistaking the expression on the colored girl's face. She had eaten the remainder of her mistress' candy, Tony thought, and this was the tragic result.

For a moment he did not move from where he was standing, then he picked up the phone and called his office. His voice was steady.

"All kinds of hell have suddenly broke, baby," he said. He related the details.

When he hung up, the wail of a siren touched his ears. He went to the door and saw the police cars swinging down the studio street. Detectives hopped out and entered the sound stage.

Tony Key flipped his cigarette away, and there was a strange light in his green eyes. Curley Conley was forcing Britton down the walk toward the dressing room.

"I want to know the reason for this!" the director demanded.

"Just a question," Tony told him. "About Miss Bow. Did she mention that anyone had visited her dressing room?"

"YES. I THINK she said—said she had seen Luke Chesterton, an old flame of hers. Although I don't remember whether she had seen him in the dressing room or on the way back from it to the set." Britton shook his head incredulously. "But why are *you* asking me these things, Swanson?"

Tony Key smiled without humor, and partially rubbed off the mask that was on his face. "Jack Swanson has been—is dead," he said quietly.

Britton looked as though his eyes would pop.

Tony nodded. "That is all. You may go back and talk to the detectives if you want."

"But who are you?"

"Just an agent," Tony said, "a movie agent who sometimes interests himself in the solution of crimes. Mr. Schmidt can probably tell you more about it."

Curly Conley asked: "What next, boss?"

"Luke Chesterton. I want to see him. I'll be at the studio commissary."

As he walked in the direction of the commissary, thoughts paraded through Tony Key's vexed mind. The events of the past few hours seemed to be jumbled and confused, with nothing to link them together. Yet he knew that somehow they *did* link, they had to all fit into their proper places, and when that was done the solution of the murders would be at hand.

Considering everything that had taken place, he tried to weigh the importance of each thing, and it occurred to him suddenly, that motive for the murders stood before everything else. Schmidt had given him Swanson's version of the card game, and a brief history of Chesterton, Borden and Brandon. He was aware that the solution must be plain from the facts he had already learned, exactly who was guilty. From the standpoint of *motive* and *alibi*, it could be only one possible person. Yet, as he walked, and thought, the name of that person was not yet in his mind.

But by the time he entered the commissary he had already mapped the course he would doggedly follow to the conclusion of the case. The counter girl, the only one present, looked up.

"Yes?"

"I'm seeking information," Tony said. "Do you remember to whom you sold candy within the past few hours?"

She shook her head. "I hope you don't think I keep a list. I must have sold a hundred bars."

Tony Key's green eyes flickered. He laid the wrapper on the counter. "It was this kind. Do you carry it?"

"Uh huh."

He named over the men, and Mrs. Swanson, described them to her. For a moment she said nothing, then at last:

"The tall one—the old bit player. I'm sure he bought that kind of a candy bar here."

"You mean Bill Borden?"

"They called him Bill," she said.

Tony Key put the candy wrapper back in his pocket. "Thanks." Just then the door slammed. "Hello!"

Tony turned, and gasped. "Betty! What the devil are you doing here?"

Betty Gale, her platinum blonde hair absolutely radiant. She was wearing a green coat, and a green tam hat, and laughed a little grimly. "You didn't think I was going to miss out on the most exciting thing since the advent of talkies, did you?"

"But I told you to stay at the office and I meant it. You're liable to be hurt around here. Besides—"

"Yeah. Besides, they might cast me in the pic to fill Myrna Bow's unhappy shoes. Mr. Schmidt just said 'Why Betty, where have you been lately?' About that time I saw Curly and he told me where I could find you."

TONY KEY'S SMOOTH face was without emotion and his lips closed tightly. He put a cigarette between them, snapped a match and lit it. "Did you bring any little message along from Curly?" he asked coldly.

"Oh, yes," she replied, "he told me to tell you that so far he hasn't been able to find Luke Chesterton; but that he is still diligently looking and will bring him the moment he can lay hands on him. Also, Los Angeles detectives seem to be galloping all over the lot, and I have just cabled Lloyd's in London, betting ten to one that Doc White's pronouncement of natural death by heart failure is going to stand up about three quarters of a minute longer."

"They haven't sent a coroner nor removed the body?"

"No. Technically, though secretly, you are still in charge of the case which oddly enough carries about two tenths of a gram of weight with them. They aren't boys who go in much for fables, however, and the bad odor of murder is already beginning to hurt their nostrils. If there is a Winchell stooge around, or one of Jimmy Fiddler's—"

Tony glanced at the girl behind the counter, then back to Betty. "Why don't you send your opinions to *Billboard*, then *everybody* will know my status!"

She gulped, flushed.

Tony Key said: "Honey baby, listen to papa just once and go and hitch hike a ride back to the office, will you?"

"But Tony, I—"

A rock flew through the window, crashed out the large over-head electric light globe. Tony Key turned toward the door, sweeping Betty Gale behind him, and going for his gun, as he saw a figure emerging through the frame of the portal.

His hand was still grappling at the shoulder holster when red belched from the doorway.

A screaming slug of lead tore through Tony Key's side.

5

The Killer Strikes

HIS BLUE STEEL automatic half-drawn, the flame of pain of a bullet that had skirted his clothing and ripped a crimson stream across his side, the world's highest paid detective had the count of eight on him at the outset of the attack. The impact of the shot spun him around, sent him reeling like a drunken man for the floor.

Key heard the girl behind the counter scream, but he could not see her; could see nothing in the combined darkness of the night and the unlighted interior of the commissary. He could only guess in that fleeting moment what was in Betty Gale's mind; how safe she now was from a stray shot, how safe she would be as this fight progressed.

He saw red flash again, heard the screaming of a bullet over his head as it thudded into the wall. Pawing at the floor, Tony Key, hot eyes desperately trying to pierce the darkness, gripped the automatic in his hand.

His finger touched the cold trigger.

Wham—Wham!

But the echo of those shots mocked him, for they echoed in a splintering of wood, and now he heard the footsteps of the figure who came toward him through the dark. Pressing his back to the wall, the pain in his side intense, Tony Key forced his legs to lift his body upright. The fire of the attacker sounded again, no more than three feet from him:

Wham!

Tony Key's shoulder first screamed in agonized protest, then went numb. He was jerked back to the wall by the impact; but even as he hit it, and once more braced himself against that wall, he heard the second scream of the counter girl, felt a greater nearness of his opponent, the impending rush forward of the other man. His finger touched twice again on the slim trigger finger of the automatic.

Wham! Wham!

But the twin blasts of hell roared from the muzzle of the steel weapon a second too late. The other man was on him, had his wrist and was pressing it down. He heard one bullet crack into the floor; although he did not hear the second. Something cried into his consciousness the significance of this, and he wondered, for an instant, how in the din of noise and fury he should be aware of his exact marksmanship. The answer was the rigid training under which he had gone in the government service.

He heard an oath break from the figure's lips. He felt a lessening of the grip on his arm, and jerking back, Tony Key forced the arm that extended from his wounded shoulder, about the attacker's neck. He pressed down with all the weight of his body in a hammer lock.

But it did not work. The shoulder was too weak. And now, his automatic wrested from his grip, and clattering to the floor, he felt a round rod jamming into his stomach. In a moment—a bare moment, that gun muzzle would spit lead, and Tony Key would be no longer.

He brought his right hand down, gripped the barrel of the other's gun; but it seemed impossible to tear it away from its deadly position in his stomach. Writhing with all the strength left in him, Tony Key managed suddenly to jerk his body to one side.

The gun crashed, missing him by an inch. It was not so dark now that he could not see the killer—at least the dark form of him—swinging in his direction. Tony Key shoved himself away from the wall as a fighter shoves himself away from the ropes. He lunged forward.

One hand on the other man's gun wrist, he bore down, and they fell to the floor together. Tony Key kept his hands wrapped about that wrist, kept trying to disarm the attacker. But his opponent suddenly rolled over. Tony's grip was torn away, and in the next instant something blunt—the butt of the gun, slashed at his forehead.

Grimly, his brain suddenly alive with pain, Tony Key tried to keep consciousness. He felt hot blood trickling down his face; felt more than ever now the bullet wounds in his shoulder and in his side. He lifted his arms, tried to writhe his body.

But the gun butt came down again—viciously.

It caught Tony on the side of the head and tore away flesh and hair; and although Tony Key fought to keep open his eyes, struggled to keep his consciousness; told himself, his mind and his heart, that he must not stop, could not stop, a surge of blackness suddenly overpowered him.

BEFORE HE OPENED his eyes; before even he knew where he was and what he had been doing, he was conscious of the serene quiet. And then he remembered—and because following the quiet there was suddenly an uproar of voices— he knew that he could have been unconscious no more than two or three minutes.

He opened his eyes at exactly the same time the lights were turned back on, and at first he could not see very well and blinked once or twice before his vision was cleared. People were bending over him, and everyone was talking at once so that he did not know what any one particular person said.

Then, in a moment—it seemed a moment—there was warm water, and someone bathing his head, and his shoulder. After a while they put him in a chair and Dr. White—who worked for Tony—came over and put temporary bandages on him. He said: "You will have to go to the hospital at once," and only shook his head when Tony Key grinned. That hard grin that a man could not argue against.

Gradually, as all this went on, Tony found out what had happened in the two minutes that he had been out of the world; and he was surprised that so many things could happen in two minutes.

Briefly, it amounted to the fact that the man with whom he had been fighting, believing him dead, had immediately rushed out of the place. Betty Gale, who during the fray had stood by helplessly, had told the counter girl—had shouted over her shoulder rather—to see that Tony was taken care of at once, and to tell him that she was going to follow the killer at a safe distance so that he would not get away.

"We saw who it was who left the commissary when a light from a sound stage across the studio street dimly reflected across his figure," the counter girl said. "That was when Betty Gale left, leaving that message."

"What did—did this man look like?" Tony asked.

The counter girl could not tell exactly. "But his hair looked very smooth—glossy, I might say."

"The shooting must have attracted attention. Didn't anyone else see him?"

"I don't know," the girl answered. "The fight between you and him all took place in—well, it couldn't have been much longer than a minute or two."

Tony Key knew that she spoke the truth, although she might have underestimated the time. A fight—especially a duel with guns—can seem an eternity although in duration it may not be more than a minute.

"And it wasn't until a couple of minutes after that that people realized something was wrong over here," she concluded.

TONY KEY GOT up, his legs unsteady beneath him. The remainder of the wax had been washed from his face, and his green eyes flickered grimly now as he made his way through the small crowd. What had taken place had left him one significant clue: his back had been turned to the window and door of the commissary at the time things started.

Wearing the clothes and wig of Jack Swanson, the killer had believed *he was Swanson! The motive of the killer in murdering Swanson was so strong that, believing himself to be unsuccessful in the first attempt, he had dared it again, in the bluntest and surest of possible ways—by gun fire!*

But, although Tony had what he believed now was the key to the solution, its importance, so far as he was concerned, was washed away by the peril in which Betty Gale had deliberately put herself. He had to take up her trail—where there was no trail—and follow her. He had to find her before the killer discovered she had been following him!

Frenzied though he now was, Tony Key realized that the only

way you came through victoriously on a baffling case was to employ every power of deduction in your possession. He still remembered the bullet he had not heard hit. The bullet he had fired from the automatic.

"Did the man who left—limp?" he asked.

"Limp?" she gasped. "He staggered, if you can call that a limp."

Suddenly Tony saw a rotund little figure who wore horn-rimmed glasses trying to push through the crowd.

"Chesterton!"

The comedian turned, eyed Tony Key's bandages in bewilderment. "Yes?"

"Looking for someone?"

"I—I heard that Jack Swanson had been hurt," Luke Chesterton said.

"You *heard* that?" Tony asked sharply. But he went on before Chesterton could answer: "Did you see a man named Conley? Curley Conley?"

"No—I—I didn't. I was out of the studio, across the street for some supper."

The inter-studio phone in the commissary rang. Tony Key waved back the counter girl, and going quickly to the instrument answered. Betty had said she would call; if this were she—!

"Hello?"

"Tony," she gasped, "I'm way out here at the end of No Man's Land; and just luckily I found a phone that is in a muddy dug-out marked Sector K."

"All right," he breathed, "stay right where you are. I'll—"

"Tony," she cut in, "are you all right?"

"Sure. I'm fine. But you won't be, when I get my hands on you. I'm going to—"

Tony Key's blood suddenly ran cold. Betty Gale was not that kind of girl who screamed easily. But at this second her shrill and terrified cry was coming through the wire. The scream was cut off. The line went dead.

6

Motive for Murder

STUNNED THOUGH HE was, Tony Key moved fast. Doc White handed him his gun, and as he raced from the commissary, he was fumbling with a new clip to put in it. He hurried over to sound stage No. 6, hopped into one of the police cars, and before the surprised detectives at the door could call out, was speeding away in it.

The studio was large and K sector, where war scenes had been filmed, was almost a half mile down the bumpy tar road that wound past set after set, huge buildings with false fronts, complete western towns; the set of a huge steamship. And as he pressed the accelerator down, Tony Key already knew who the killer was.

The chain of events, the circumstances surrounding the activities of every suspect, coupled with the most important thing of all—the motive, clearly indicated it could be one person and one person only.

He reached the patchy land that was supposed to represent a shell torn battle field. The road ended here, but Tony Key kept on driving. The car bounced on its springs, almost shook him loose from the wheel.

Then—in the distance ahead—he saw a figure silhouetted in the yellow glare of the headlights. The figure of a man carrying a girl—Betty Gale. He saw another car—a roadster.

Clinging to the wheel of his own car, the motor humming

red hot, he raced the machine forward.

Tony Key was out of the car the moment it began to slow down, in its crazy, wild course. He stumbled across the ground, aware that his side had begun bleeding again; aware that there was a terrible painful pounding in his head. But he vowed that this time the killer was not going to get away from him. He drew his blue steel automatic.

"Don't move," snapped Tony, "you're covered!" Key moved forward, brought out handcuffs and slapped them on his prisoner.

Laughing—something in his chest made him laugh because Betty Gale, terrified though she had been, could keep her sense of humor.

He saw her grin, "A letter from Garcia, boss."

She handed him a packet of bills in an envelope on which were the initials "M.B."

"He—the killer—had this?"

She nodded. "It came out of his pocket while I was trying to keep him from hitting me with the butt of that gun he had. Myrna Bow must have left it out here for him—which was the reason he had to come here before leaving the lot."

"That finishes the case," Tony Key said softly.

Betty Gale said: "It *almost* finished me."

THE ROOM IN the old Los Angeles court house was filled with people—the detectives, the District Attorney. Also Sam Schmidt, smoking a short cigar; Ann Swanson, looking more reposed now, even pretty, softly weeping; Luke Chesterton, looking very pale and not wearing his horn-rimmed glasses; Bill Borden, tall, slim, his wrinkled face set; and Percy Brandon, a strange light in his young eyes. Morning sunshine splashed through the dusty windows.

Tony Key stood beside his platinum blonde secretary and saw all of them. Slowly, he moved forward, as Betty Gale opened her note book.

Tony put a cigarette between his lips and lit it; his green eyes flickered. "The motive was the main clue to these crimes," he said, "motive and the actions of the suspects. Carefully checking both of these and even completely disregarding all other evidence, it is quite clear that Bill Borden murdered both Jack Swanson and Myrna Bow."

Bill Borden, his gray hair lying very flat, his sallow face without expression, stood handcuffed, and flanked by two detectives. He stared straight ahead, and past Tony Key.

"Being only an extra and bit player when he *did* work—which was seldom," Tony continued, "he was desperate for money. Like a lot of others who get Hollywood in their blood, he liked to, felt he had to, live high.

"He had once tried to blackmail Jack Swanson, and now—trying the same thing on Myrna Bow—he was sure that from watching his actions during work on *Pride of the Nation,* Swanson had guessed what he was up to. Yet Swanson was not one to butt into affairs not his own, and his scruples not being the Sunday School kind, he figured it was a pretty good bet that Swanson would not voice his suspicion.

"Not until Jack Swanson lost so heavily in the card games. When Swanson got up from the table, both Luke Chesterton and Percy Brandon were called on the set for a shot, *and were occupied for at least twenty minutes. The twenty minutes during which Swanson was killed.* Borden mentioned this himself when I impersonated Swanson and came back to the table, although he stated that he *had remained at the table,* when as a matter of fact, I learned he had gotten up in disgust and *walked away* when he drew a blank hand in the four hundred dollar pot!

"He saw Swanson leave the sound stage and go to Schmidt's office. About to shake money successfully out of Myrna Bow, Bill Borden's desperate mind told him that Swanson could be going to Schmidt for one reason only—to make a loan. And since Swanson and Schmidt were not friendly it occurred to him that the only way Swanson, bitter that he had lost his money, could get a loan would be to reveal the blackmail racket that was taking place right on the lot. So he went to the open window and threw the knife which, although he didn't know it and tried to kill me later because he thought *I* was Swanson, proved fatal to the old actor."

Tony Key dropped his cigarette and stepped on it. The room was hot, and he opened his collar. The silence was oppressive.

He went on: "Then into a murder set-up, Bill Borden did some fast thinking. He wrote the death note which he raced over to Swanson's house and left—to make it look as though Schmidt had committed the crimes in revenge for Swanson's taking his wife ten years ago.

"He returned to the studio, and by this time he was panic stricken. He thought of the conversation at cards and Chesterton's past love affair with Myrna Bow, and his hatred for Jack Swanson.

"The finger of suspicion, he thought, would point to Chesterton too, if he killed Myrna Bow.

"WITH HER DEAD, he would not only have the money she delivered, but be sure she didn't break down someday and tell on him. He was more afraid of her telling than before, because of Swanson's murder. He went to the commissary, bought a bar of candy, poisoned it. He knew Myrna Bow's love for candy but that she got little of it because of her diet. He probably bribed the maid to see that she got this particular piece. The maid was unsuspecting and died too, according to Borden's plan.

"All of this he was able to accomplish in little more than a half hour, after which he returned to the card game, believing the murders had been executed without flaw, and that no suspicion would be directed upon himself.

"*But,* for reasons I have stated, Chesterton and Brandon were exonerated from suspicion, leaving only Sam Schmidt, who—although he may have had motive for killing Swanson—*would not* have motive for poisoning Myrna Bow and her maid. Therefore, Bill Borden's careful planning, instead of hiding him, lead straight to his door!"

Tony paused, sucked in his breath, and looked at the sea of faces in front of him. Eyes staring, the sun coming in through the dusty window. His voice lower, he concluded: "When Borden mistook me for Swanson, and attacked me, he got a bullet through his leg.

That wound is my final evidence, gentlemen. And my final plea is that you allow the press stories Miss Betty Gale has written, to be released, instead of giving the reporters your own versions. It will be best that way."

The tension broke, there was the drone of voices, everyone talking at once. Tony Key sat down in a chair, exhausted;

he wiped sweat from his face and lit another cigarette. He was conscious of people milling everywhere: Bill Borden, face white, being taken out; Luke Chesterton, as he departed, his face very pale; Percy Brandon offering the money Jack Swanson had lost, to Ann Swanson, and Sam Schmidt, his face somehow very light, as though transformed, refusing the money and putting his arm about Ann Swanson's shoulders. It was all part of the aftermath of a tough case; part of the human drama of Hollywood.

These things that happened in this old court room, the world's highest paid detective saw; and he knew that his job was over, and that pretty soon he would have to get back to the office. Then he was aware of Betty Gale beside him.

"Let's relax, boss," she said. "I know where the new Charlie Chan pic is playing, and they say it's box office sugar. Want to go?"

Murder Game—With Mirrors

*Tony Key Couldn't Prevent a Man From
Keeping a Death Date—But He Could
Tell You Why, How and With Whom!*

THE YOUNG MAN stepped off the elevator on the third floor and paused to light a cigarette. An office girl glanced at him in passing, then turned and looked again. The young man puffed on the cigarette, his eyes shifting nervously. He was handsome; garbed in white flannels, blue jacket, and two-toned shoes. He had a mop of curly blond hair and large gray eyes. There was a frightened gleam in those eyes now and something unsteady in his gait as he started down the marble floor.

He stopped in front of a frosted glass door, dropped the cigarette and stepped on it. He glanced at the words written on the glass, a cold smile touching his lips. "*Tony Key*" it said, "*Arists' Representative, Motion Pictures.*" He turned the knob and walked in.

The outer office was elegantly furnished, with a deep rug into which the man's feet sank; with the finest of modernistic furniture. And it all looked very new—because the furniture was seldom used; people just didn't hang around in *this* office to wait for anybody. Through a small window at the end of the waiting room a platinum blonde sat at a typewriter, and now she turned and snapped back the window. The young man sucked in his breath. He was used to beautiful women in Hollywood, where they came ten cents a dozen, but there was something startling about this girl's beauty. The deep blue of her eyes, the way her blonde-white hair glistened in contrast with the black patent leather dress she wore; the way the soft red of her lips accentuated the velvety smoothness of her skin.

She looked at him a moment, then said: "Terry Fife, juvenile third lead, now working in a South Sea pic that's being shot on a relic out here in San Pedro. Good morning, Mr. Fife."

He did not smile. "You have the history of everyone in Hollywood at the tips of your fingers, haven't you, Miss Gale?"

Her blue eyes flickered. "Not everyone," she said diplomatically, "but one couldn't miss you, Mr. Fife. I saw you in a program quickie the other night and the impression was a lasting one."

He flashed white teeth. "Well, isn't that just too nice? Skip the chatter—I'm here to see Tony Key."

"I'm sorry, Mr. Fife, but he's out of town. I know he would like to see you. Having agent trouble?"

"Listen, sister," young Fife snapped, "you're not kidding me one minute. Key isn't an agent. This place is a blind, because his investigations are supposed to be secret. Keeps Hollywood crime news out of the papers. What Key is, is an ex G-man, and at present the world's highest paid detective."

The warmth left her face. "Mr. Key is not seeing anyone," she said coldly.

"Yes he is. This is once you happened to be mistaken. He's seeing me." He lifted a blue automatic from his coat pocket and held it levelled at her. "All right," he went on, "don't sit there and gape, tell him I want to see him!"

Betty Gale looked calmly down at the gun, then she got to her feet, straightened the black dress about her shapely hips, and disappeared.

TONY KEY HAD dark, smoothly combed hair, and eyes that were as hard as green jade. He was throwing darts at a

*Tip Martin started for his
gun—changed his mind*

target when Betty entered.

"Hello, sweetheart," he said.

"Tony," she cut in, "Curly Conley is downstairs, isn't he? Well, there's a young ham out in the reception room that has a bad odor and a gun. I suggest he be clipped, wrapped in cellophane and sent back to Paramet Studio C.O.D."

"Has he really a bad odor?"

"I wouldn't know," she replied, "but I'll bet his acting has, and if you think this is funny, it isn't. Some one of the six moguls who knows your true occupation has whispered in his ear that you aren't an agent."

Tony Key cocked his right eyebrow. "Now it's getting serious. What's his name?"

"Terry Fife."

For a moment Key was silent. He went to the window and looked down on Hollywood Boulevard, rubbed his jaw. "Betty," he said without turning, "I haven't told you yet—intended to today. Somebody has been shaking Fife down. Lately he has received threats on his life. It's been all I could do to keep the stories out of the papers. It's against policy, but you'd better send him in."

For a moment she did not speak, then: "Keeping secrets from your first lieutenant. Next you'll be wanting your engagement ring back." With that she left the office, slamming the door.

Tony Key tapped a cigarette on his thumbnail, turned as Fife came in, gun still in hand.

"Sit down."

"I think I'll stand," said Fife. "Pretty damn snooty for a detective, aren't you?"

Key asked coldly: "Did you come here for help, or do you want a swat in the face? I said put that gun away and sit down— and I'm not a very patient man!"

Fife stared for a moment, then slipped the automatic into his pocket and sank down in a chair. He wiped sweat from his face.

"You know all the details, don't you?" he whispered. "Somebody shaking money out of me—and now a threat of death." His voice picked up, but he seemed to be choking. "I don't know who it is. Naturally, I've got enemies. Who hasn't? But I don't know who'd want to kill me. I'm scared. Damned scared. I begged Mr. Fuller to tell me who had been squashing the cases around the studios so I could appeal to you personally. God, my career has just started. I don't want to die!"

Key picked up another dart and threw it at the target. "What are the latest developments?"

"A phone call this time instead of a note," Fife said excitedly. "A voice that was obviously disguised. It said I would die within the next twenty-four hours—no matter where I was! Why can't we call in the police? Lord, Key, I don't want to—to—"

"The police are fully acquainted with the case," Tony Key said, "and they've a couple of men working on it. But until I throw in the sponge and admit it is too much for me, they're naturally giving me full sway. My business, Mr. Fife, varies from that of a private detective. You must remember I used to be a federal agent, and my work here is both for the good of motion pictures and the law. A *specialist* in movie cases." He threw another dart. "You're working aboard a relic sailing ship now?"

The sweat continued to come and Fife was wiping it from his face with a handkerchief. "Yes—that's right."

KEY WENT TO the target and gathered the darts in his hand. He glanced back. "When you started getting shake-down demands—from a gentleman I believe to be Tip Martin," he said slowly, "I did a little research into your immediate past. And since this is so serious, you must forgive me if I mention unpleasantries."

"Sure—sure, that's all right."

"There was an ingenue named Molly O'Hara," Tony Key went on. He was backing now to get aim on the target, not looking at the actor. "She was a pretty sweet kid, they say—big future and all that. Then there was some talk about her heart being broken. Worse: that her faithless romeo bragged of it so much her career was badly damaged. Gossip columns. Loose tongues. When her option expired—"

Terry Fife leaped to his feet. "I know what you're driving at! But it isn't true. Those stories were exaggerated. Molly—well,

Molly still considers me her friend, I'm sure. Just yesterday I took her brother out to the ship to watch some shots. He's going out with me again tomorrow. Hell, Tom O'Hara and I were classmates, we—"

Key shrugged. "I was aware that was a tender spot, and it was worth a thought. Forget it." He threw another dart, hitting the bull's-eye.

Fife watched him for a moment, then: "For the love of God, will you quit doing that? They say you're the highest paid detective in the world! Well, my life is in danger. Why don't you trace down this Tip Martin, or whatever his name is? *He's* the one who is behind it! I don't want to die! *Do something!*"

Tony Key glanced at him, his face set. "You know more about the prospects of your own murder. There are, naturally, things you haven't told me—and I agree that there is a great possibility Tip Martin may, for one reason or another, want to kill you. He's a clever man. Owns a gambling club, and probably gets away with more blackmail than any crook in the world."

"Well, why don't you—"

Tony Key showed him his hand. "With men like Martin you *just* don't. He's got enough protection to keep the Japs out of California. Smart shysters, a way of doing things—"

"You mean," Fife gasped, "I have to die merely because some—"

Key shook his head. "I mean just this: I'm one man. I have assistants, but they all work directly with or under me. We can travel only one road at a time, particularly when every moment appears to be so important. *I* was going to investigate the O'Hara angle and save Martin for a bigger build up. But if you think Martin is the one—"

52 / Steve Fisher

"I *know it!*"

"All right," Key said quietly, "then that's that. I can tell you what I think will keep you alive—and I can promise that you'll have no trouble from Martin. That is, I'll watch him closely enough to assure you of safety. Meanwhile, you move to a hotel. Hollywood Hall, I suggest. Tell *no one* of this change. I'll keep in touch with you."

Fife was visibly shaken. "Just as you say."

Tony Key scrutinized the young actor carefully. Then, laying the darts on the desk, he said, "All right. Wait here a moment." He left, entering Betty Gale's small office. As she looked up, he told her: "Get Curly Conley at once. Have him tail Fife. He's to act as body guard in case anyone gets rough. Also get hold of White. I'll want his company later."

Her delicate eyebrows were raised. "As bad as that?"

He nodded. "It's plenty bad. Did you do your usual checking up while Fife and I were talking?"

Her blue eyes were bright. "Uh huh. All the data. Fife's option is up next month. His only starring role was in a program quickie that laid an egg. But Fife had enough syrup for fans in the sticks, and they've screamed so loud to put him in something decent the moguls are considering it. If that makes anything—and I think it does—there you are."

Tony grinned. "Yeah, the leading and current sweet boy at Fife's studio might be getting jealous. But it's too vague to look at. Besides, Fife has the notion that shake-down artist, Tip Martin, is the nasty gentleman involved. And sweetheart, the idea of taking a look-in at Martin pleases me. The slick rat has tied my hands with alibis and shysters for months."

She scowled. "Martin is the kind of baby who is liable to tie more than your hands, Tony. I mean: legs and arms, then tossing you into the *LaBrea* pits or somewhere."

Tony Key's smooth face was inscrutable, his green eyes like jade. "That's why I'm going to see him," he said.

THE ORCHESTRA WAS playing a new number. Soft lights were shifting across the smooth faces of dancing couples. Stars, extras, and business people sat about at tables. Some of them looked up as the huge ex-wrestler, Tip Martin, clad in a tan top coat and felt hat, swung down the aisle, two unsympathetic looking gentlemen at his heels.

Martin entered his office and closed the door. The tuxedo garbed pair who had followed remained outside. Each of their tailor-made dinner coats bulged in the vicinity of the shoulder pit. Neither of them were smiling.

Inside the darkened office, Martin snapped on a lamp over his desk and sat down. His nose had been broken and it looked as though it had been smashed back into his scarred face. His eyes were spots of black that glittered with a hard, cold light. Like many who lived in the film capitol, he had done his time in pictures—small and violent parts where he choked men, for screen purposes, until they were dead, or propped a machine-gun into a faked window sill and burned down G-men. But he had worked all too infrequently and had given up the screen career for shadier enterprises, which had grown profitably in the passing months.

He picked up the phone now. "Operator," he said in a thick voice. "I want Wyoming 6 1 2—"

Then—his voice caught in his throat, broke off. Slowly, he placed the hand phone back in its receiver and stared through the light of his desk lamp at a man who had silently stepped from the shadows in the far corner of the room. A smooth young man, with boring green eyes, who held in his hand an unpleasant looking little automatic.

"Hello, Tip," the young man said quietly, a cool smile on his inscrutable face, "you're in late."

Tip Martin started for his gun, read death in the other's eyes, changed his mind. He put his hands on the glass top of the desk and leaned forward. "What do you want here, Tony Key?"

Key kept the gun level. "I'm taking over a little matter of life and death for a friend of mine. You'll pardon the intrusion—I hope."

Martin's eyes glittered. "I thought you were an agent."

Tony Key was still smiling. "Most people are supposed to think that, but a long while ago you took the trouble of finding out that I wasn't. You don't miss any tricks, Martin. Well, neither do I."

"You seem to be looking for trouble."

Key shook his head. "On the other hand, I'm seeking to avoid it. I've made the discovery, never mind how, that Fife called you and threatened to expose your shake-down racket."

Tip Martin laughed harshly. "What does that mean? You're snooping for nothing, Key. Fife can go to court any time he wants and it's all right with me." A crafty light crossed his face. "Any time he wants—if he thinks he's got something to tell."

"You cover up pretty well, don't you?"

"Sure."

Key gripped the gun a little tighter. "I'm hanging around. So are a couple of my friends, and two or three L.A. dicks. Thought I'd tell you so you can cancel Fife's murder, if it's slated for tonight."

"Murder?"

"You heard me," Tony Key said softly. He slipped the gun into his pocket, put a cigarette between his lips and lit it. Martin's gun came out at once. Key walked to the door without looking at it. "And I wouldn't start things here, Martin, not now anyway. I covered you when you came in to keep you from any impulsive moves you might have been sorry for later." His hand was on the knob of the door now.

TIP MARTIN LEAPED to his feet, his ugly face livid with rage. "Damn you, Key," he breathed, "I don't know what kind of a game you think you're playing, but whatever it is, you're all wrong. But I'll tell you this, and you can think about it: so long as you're gonna try to include me in your smart-aleck detective clean up of this town, you can expect plenty from me. I've never muscled in on your racket of cracking murders and snatches, but if you muscle into *my* business, or whatever you think my business is, one of us is going for a ride in a hearse down Hollywood Boulevard!"

"That's food for thought," Tony Key said softly, "because I'm going to work on you until I blast your rotten racket wide open."

He opened the door and stepped out of the office. The two questionable gentleman garbed in tuxedos stared at him in surprise. One of them grabbed his arm, but a moment later let it go. Tony walked over to a table and sat down. Betty Gale, wearing a shimmering blue evening gown that clung tightly about her slim figure and shone in contrast with the platinum blonde of her hair, glanced at him.

"Had a long wait for Martin, didn't you, boss. Where had he been?"

"Don't know," Tony replied.

At that moment he saw Molly O'Hara enter through the revolving doors of the club, and with her was a tall young man—her brother, Tom O'Hara. Tom was handing the hat check girl his wraps when another man entered, joining the party.

"Look, Betty," Key said, "the O'Haras, and Glen Manners."

"Not Glen Manners," she replied, "you mean Heart Throb Glen Manners, whom God hears about in young maidens' prayers."

The two men and the red-haired girl were taken to a nearby table and seated. They were so close Key could hear Manners' smooth voice.

"Nice that we arrived here at the same time, isn't it, Molly?" He looked at his wrist watch. "Didn't know if I'd be able to make it by ten. But as I drove up, there you and Tom were, just coming in—"

Tom O'Hara, a blond youth who had starred in several Coast football games a few years ago, seemed to be nervous. "As a matter of fact," he said, "we almost failed to come ourselves." He laughed hollowly. "Didn't we, Molly?"

The red-haired girl nodded soberly and said, "Yes—we did."

The music started again. Betty Gale smiled at Tony. "I know we're here on business and all that, boss, but what about exercising the gams?"

"Sure," Key said, and got up.

They had just started dancing when Tony spotted Max White, who was both his make-up expert and henchman, rushing past the tables to get to him. He stepped off the dance floor. White arrived breathless.

"Curly Conley's in the hospital. Somebody cracked him on the head. He managed to crawl to where somebody would call an ambulance and now he's having a devil of a time stalling the cops about what happened to him. Says he can't hold out much longer, but he wants you to get there first!"

"Get where?"

"Terry Fife's house."

"Then he didn't move to a hotel?"

White looked blank. "I guess not. Conley said he's—he's been murdered!"

Tony Key blanched. He said: "This is a helluva thing. Take Betty home, White. Do you know how long ago all this happened?"

"Well, Curly was out for a while. It must have been more than an hour."

"Oh, my Lord," Tony breathed, and headed for the door.

TERRY FIFE'S MODERATE home was in the hills of Hollywoodland. Tony found the body on an enclosed second floor porch. The rest of the house was empty, and outside Tony could hear rain falling on the clay road, across the roof. He put on the porch lights and looked down.

Fife lay, white-faced, eyes bulging, mouth partly open. A stream of hardened blood had trickled down across his jaw and onto the floor. The back of his head had been bashed in, possibly from being crashed on the floor. But the most hideous mark of all was the appearance of his neck. It was blue, and bloated, as though he had been strangled by an enraged gorilla.

Tony Key examined the neck briefly, and then got to his feet. He lighted a cigarette and listened to the falling of the rain. At last he moved to the screen and looked down at the road. He remained there until he saw the police car drive up the winding pass, followed by the machine of the coroner. There was no apparent sign of struggle except an overturned chair and the wrinkled carpet.

Tony waited until the police came up, spoke with them briefly, and left the house.

Things hadn't turned out so well. The murder had occurred around nine, and neither the O'Haras nor Tip Martin had come into the club until after ten. Tony had known enough then to expect trouble, but he thought if Fife had moved to the hotel, in accordance with his instructions, he would have been safe. But Fife had remained here, for some reason, and even the strong arm of Curly Conley had been unable to save him.

The worst of it was, Tony Key had his suspects lined up, practically sitting in his lap, but he had no idea which way to point his finger for an accusation that would last longer than it would take the accused to scream denial.

He had looked for clues and found none, and now he must consider the essentials of the crime, the type of murder. Fife could have died either from concussion or strangulation, which proved what?

Key was about to climb into his roadster when he paused. Proved what? Hell, it was a lead. Right in front of his eyes.

He slammed the door of the car shut and began looking around. He had a notion that if there had been a murder instrument the killer wouldn't have been foolish enough to carry it with him, even though he had not left it in the house. That too, might have been for a reason—not leaving the murder weapon in the house.

With the aid of a flashlight he searched the road, through the brush at the side of it. The cops left, the coroner took away the body. Still Tony Key, his clothing drenched with rain, stayed and searched. His theory was the only thing that was going to crack the case, if it was to be cracked. But it was beginning to look as though the theory was little more than a wrong guess.

Suddenly, however, the beams of his light stopped on something that glistened with crimson. He broke through the weeds on the side of the hill and picked it up. It was a bent lead pipe, and it was very bloody.

Tony Key smiled through the falling rain.

IT WAS STILL raining the next day when he climbed aboard the relic sailing ship that was anchored just outside the San Pedro breakwater. The movies were using it to shoot a picture in which Terry Fife had had a part.

A package wrapped in oil cloths tucked under his arm, Tony Key crossed the deck. He saw the dim figures of the battle fleet in the distance—sleek gray battleships cruising to sea, aircraft carriers swinging quietly at anchor. On this vessel he felt the list, saw the heavy timber masts sway in the wind and rain, and heard the groan of the bulkheads as the craft swung back and forth in the current.

He went below to where the company was shooting. Molly O'Hara had no part in the film, but she and her brother Tom were aboard at the request of the picture producers. The producers had acted on orders from Key. Tony saw the slim, blond young man and the red-haired girl now as he neared the "brig" set. The large sound cameras were set up, and heavy arc lights were just beginning to come on. An actor was chained down, and Glen Manners, the star, was ready to make an entrance as soon as the scene began.

Tony Key stood back behind the camera with the director. Betty Gale, who had been on the other side of the room, spotted him. She came at once.

"Tony—" she started to say.

But at that moment the clappers that marked the shot snapped. There was intense silence. Betty's pretty red mouth closed and remained closed. She stood at Tony's side watching the scene. Glen Manners strode before the cameras. The actor chained on his back looked up at him pleadingly, and the dialogue began. In seventy-five seconds the shot was finished. The powerful klieg lamps started going off.

"Everything's okay amidships," Betty Gale whispered. The platinum blonde was garbed in a light green sweater and a skirt of a darker green, both of which invited a second glance.

"Then you got Clare, the spider girl in Culver's sideshow, to show the carpenters how to set everything up?"

She nodded.

Tony Key stepped forward and spoke to the director. Silence was called by the director and echoed by four of his assistants, one after another in order of their importance. Every one on the set was asked to listen to what Key had to say.

Tony smiled affably. "It isn't much," he said, as though he were apologizing, "and then again, it may be. As most of you know, I'm only an agent for actors and writers, but there is a matter in which I happened to make what may be a curious discovery. Your boss has asked me to get your cooperation in attempting to prove my theory before we inform the police and cause unnecessary trouble."

He unwrapped the oilcloth and brought out the bloody pipe. His voice became a little more tense. "I believe Terry Fife was murdered with this," he went on, "yet the fingerprints found on it are those of no known criminal." He smiled again. "To save you all embarrassment and police investigation, your employer wants me to get fingerprints from each of you so that they might be compared with these on the pipe. It is just possible that someone among us committed the murder. To be absolutely fair I must insist that *everyone* submit to the fingerprint test. You see, this pipe is evidence enough to hang the killer."

As he finished no one spoke. Actors, carpenters, the assistants all stared at one another.

"I'll be in the wardroom adjoining the main mess room amidships," Tony went on, "and I'll be ready for some of you in about—say—fifteen minutes."

With that, he departed.

THE PORTHOLES WERE closed and shaded so that the little wardroom was dark save for a flickering yellow lamp Tony Key had lighted and put on the table beside him. Shadows stood on every side of the room. Tony Key was seated on the table, the pipe at his elbow.

He looked at his watch and waited for time to pass. His green eyes were hard, and his heart was beating just a little faster. Three minutes had gone by when the wardroom door opened. A figure stood half shrouded in the shadows. The door closed and the figure moved forward. It was the handsome star Glen Manners, and there was a gun gripped in his hand.

"I'll have that pipe, Key," he said softly, "I think it'll look better out that porthole."

Tony Key smiled and shook his head. He pushed off the edge of the table. "I don't think so, bright boy. I think, instead, I'm going to lock you up for murder."

The star's handsome face was set. "You insolent pup," he whispered, gripping the gun tighter, "you've asked for it, and you're going to get it. Right through the stomach!"

Tony Key kept smiling. "I don't think so," he said. "The trouble is, Manners, I've been a couple of jumps ahead of you all the time. That was crude—murdering Fife with a smack on the head with a pipe, then crushing his neck black and blue with the bent pipe. You thought you could lead me to suspect that Tip Martin and his strong fingers had choked Fife to death. That since you had phoned Martin's office and told him—in the guise of Fife—that you were going to expose him, Martin would have plenty of motive, too. The swollen neck and that motive was supposed to put you in the clear. But if Martin had done it, he wouldn't have had to crack Fife on the back of the head. Your plan to throw the suspicion the other way was a boomerang that's going to put a rope around your neck!"

"I don't think so," Glen Manners whispered, "I'll tell you why, Key. Because I'm going to shoot you full of holes and get out of here—then no one up front will know who did it. I'll be back in plenty of time, and with a neat alibi. So you can gloat over your deducing in hell. As for Fife, I'm not sorry for what I did. Any man who'd treat Molly O'Hara as he did, and talk of her the way he did—"

Tony Key leaned back against the table. "That wasn't what worried you most, though, was it? What worried you was that the moguls were beginning to see Fife as syrup that one day might replace you as the great screen lover. You've been around too long as it is and—"

"Damn you and your raving!"

Tony Key's smile had not vanished. His hands were empty. "Go ahead and shoot, fair-haired boy, if you've nerve enough—"

Lips a thin line, Glen Manners pumped the trigger of the gun. Six shots roared from it in quick, deafening succession. The bullets screamed through the room. There was a horrible tinkling, and then a crashing of glass.

Tony, from an angle of the room opposite that in which Manners had seen him, rushed forward. He grasped the gun hand, and gripping Manners' wrist, swung him over his back. The actor thudded to the floor, kicking and squirming. Tony Key landed on him. His fist drove into Manners' face, and as the star shook his head, Key's other fist smashed down.

In a moment he had the handcuffs about Manners' wrists and was dragging him to his feet.

BETTY GALE STEPPED in from the main mess room, the picture director behind her. The struggle had been so brief that neither had been able to get in to help. The platinum blonde was closing a note book.

"Got every word of it, boss."

Glen Manners was staring incredulously at the broken glass. "What—how—"

"As I mentioned just a little while ago," Tony Key said, "your trouble has been that we were a couple of jumps ahead of you. You thought you saw me standing in front of you, but I wasn't there at all. Trick looking glasses, furnished us by the spider girl—Clare—who does her act that way too. What you saw was my reflection. You see, there isn't a table where you thought. It's over here, curtained off and at angles so that it looked as though it was right in front of you. It's all done with mirrors."

Glen Manners gasped. "Then you've tricked—"

Tony Key nodded, his green eyes flickering. "Had to. You see, the rain destroyed whatever fingerprints there might have been on that lead pipe. There was rain and mud—and blood. But we couldn't find fingerprints. So we had to bait the killer into what we might call the spider room so he could expose himself. And seeing I had no chance to shoot you, you did the exposing very well, Manners. I thought you would."

Manners could not speak.

"It looks, Tony," platinum Betty Gale said, "that the movies have wasted a lot of film footage. What I mean is: they're going to have to start this pic all over again. Maybe *you'd* like to be the star."

"No, thanks," said Tony Key.

"Batten Down That Killer!"

When He Felt the Handshake of Guilt,
Tony Key Knew Who Was Dealing Death
on That Giant Aircraft Carrier!

1

WHEN THE SPEED boat moved past the Honolulu breakwater he saw the giant hulk of the *Lexington* on the horizon ahead, her seventy-five planes resting on the expansive flight deck, her stacks belching smoke, and it amused him to think of a ship so huge and costly standing still in the water waiting for him to come aboard. Because a long time ago he had gone to Annapolis, and he had been an officer, and when he had resigned all of them had loathed him. He had deliberately been an hour late because it gave him pleasure to think of the captain fuming and the navigator mumbling under his breath, and the rest of the fleet lying out in LaHaina Roads, Maui, waiting too, wondering were the *Lexington* was.

He smiled and puffed at a cigarette. Of course his director would not like it too well either; nor the fat producer. They always made fools of themselves going out of their way to be nice whenever the navy permitted them to make pictures aboard ship. But neither his director nor producer could say much to William Crossett. His name in lights meant cash in box offices and there were plenty of other companies waiting to grab him up.

But as he kept watching the *Lexington* something cold and unpleasant shuddered through him, and for the first time in his life he felt as though he were a man going backward. He threw the cigarette away and shifted a little uncomfortably. He tried to purge his mind of the nostalgia of his youthful emotional hysteria, the kind he had known in Annapolis. The kind he had afterward called rot.

Crossett stopped him. His face was livid. "You're crazy if you think I'm going in there!" he said

But as the boat sped through the water and the *Lexington* loomed bigger, the horror of his past crowded deeper and deeper in his mind, and it occurred to him now that this would be the first time he had been aboard a navy boat since he had resigned. Perhaps that was the reason for his feeling and it would wear off. He would become himself again and thrust the spear of his success into the hearts of the men who gave their lives to the sea. He would pretend as though they were all ship-mates as they had once been, but he would be careful to say things that would show them the futility of their drab existence. He would mention life in Hollywood, and casually let them know the staggering weekly salary he had collected now for six consecutive years.

Yet his ambition to do this, for a while riding high, now was flagging. He was terrified. His old fear, the one he had fought through Annapolis, came choking up through his chest. The fear of guns and planes and regulation. He was afraid of the ship. He could not understand what had come over him. He was suddenly looking at his whole life as though he were not William Crossett but somebody else. Someone who stood back and viewed the whole thing from the very beginning. Someone who knew the thoughts that had been in his mind. The schemes of intrigue and treachery; his methods of cold and selfish ruthlessness.

And now he was frightened that they would not see him as the great William Crossett, but the weakling of his class, the cheat among gentlemen; the man who had not what it took to be a sailor. He looked at the uniform he wore. Neatly tailored, and glistening white, with gold wings over his chest. In stage clothes he was a lieutenant-commander. He leaned forward and kept watching the *Lexington* and he was conscious suddenly of the beating of his heart.

Desperately, as the man who stood on the side and viewed his life, he tried to find reason and quality; but there was none. Not a shred, nor had there been any since the beginning. He had pleaded with Senator Hall to appoint him to Annapolis because he thought a uniform was glamorous, and he remembered with the shame the flagitious lies he had told to convince the Senator he wanted to be a great naval officer. And from that time on he had glibly lied his way through life.

HE HAD NOT thought of it like this before because he had been able to delude himself that everything he did was right, and he had made up excuses for even the most cruel of his acts. Like Martha. It was not pleasant to think of Martha now because she was the ex-wife of one of the officers and he would soon have to face the man and shake hands with him as though they were friends.

Water splashed about the stern of the boat where he sat in cushions, and he wiped his face with a handkerchief and did not look at the *Lexington* any longer because they were too close to it. He looked at the handkerchief. There was sweat on it. He laughed, but the laughter made no sound over the motor of the boat.

"I am being a fool," he said aloud. "I will be the most celebrated man they ever had aboard, and they'll be glad enough to forget. They'll honor me."

But he was aware that even as he spoke the words, he would not be talking aloud to himself if he were not more frightened than he had ever been before in his life. He saw the side of the ship in a blur of gray before his eyes. He saw the white gangway. The boat swished alongside.

Two sailors stood at the bottom of the gangway to help him aboard, and he was trembling as they lifted him to the platform. He climbed the ladder quickly to top side. There were no side boys, no officers. Only the producer waddling across toward him.

"Well, I must say, Crossett, you took your time."

"Sorry," he murmured. "I was held up."

The producer took a cigar out of his mouth. "Yes? Well you're going to be held up once too often some of these days. Do you realize—"

William Crossett lifted his hand. "Please! I'm in no mood for your banter. Where is the first shot?"

"We were going to take one on the bridge, but it's all off now." He turned. "Mr. Johnson."

Crossett suddenly saw Tom Johnson step from a hatch and move across the deck. He swallowed as he saw the gray at Johnson's temples, the deep lines in his face, and the lieutenant-commander bars on his shoulder straps. He tried to smile, and put out his hand. His whole body was trembling.

"Well, if it isn't good old Tom!"

Johnson shook his hand, though he did not press it, and he said: "It's good to see you again, Bill. How's everything?"

The question was pointless; born of confusion and embarrassment. "All right," Crossett answered. "And you?"

"Oh—all right," Johnson said quietly. "Want to come below? We're having coffee in the wardroom."

Crossett could feel the stiffness in Johnson's voice, and he detected a coolness in his manner that might have been sheer hatred. There was no cheering. No congratulations upon his screen success. He had the feeling that he was in for something he did not expect.

"Coffee's what I need right now, Tom," he said.

The producer left them, and they went below. Tom Johnson walked a pace ahead, as though he disliked walking with Crossett. For quite a long while as they moved through the compartments he said nothing. Then:

"Martha's here. Since this is a cruise for the movies, the admiral let her come along."

For a moment the meaning of the words did not hit him, but when they did, Crossett stopped; he caught his breath. All bets were off now, the cards were on the table. He looked at Johnson through burning eyes.

"I don't quite know what you mean."

"I mean that Martha is here," Johnson said quietly.

Crossett shook his head. "But she isn't even divorced from me yet."

"Yes she is. She got a decree in another state instead of waiting a year in California. We're together again."

For a moment Crossett could not speak; his throat seemed parched. "You mean—"

"She came back to me," said Johnson.

CROSSETT SAGGED, ALMOST visibly. Of course she would come back. She had always loved Tom. Divorcing Tom, and marrying him, had been impossible madness. He had won Martha with glamor and intrigue; not because he loved her, but because she was beautiful and the navy was proud of her, as Tom Johnson had been proud of her; and William Crossett's great rotten ego, wounded that the navy would have none of him, won her, and married her because he had wanted to show them he was better than they.

But that was not what bothered him. It was that he and Martha had not gotten on well, and once or twice in drunken rage he had hit her, and another time he had thrown her down a flight of steps so that she was in bed a week. She had stuck to him through that because she had a fierce determination to make a go of the marriage; because she too had pride and it had been disgrace and shame enough that she divorced Tom—without letting the world know, through the eyes of the hungry press, that she could not stay married to William Crossett either. But she represented the navy he hated, and he had been utterly rotten with her. He had wanted to make her suffer. It was a quirk in his nature. The selfish revenge of wounded vanity. And at last when he had crushed all the pride and respect out of her, he had come home from location one day to find her gone. He had laughed when he read her note. He had been cruelly satisfied. The turn of events rounded out the plans he had made from the beginning.

And now Tom Johnson was saying softly, "She came back to me," and in a few minutes he was going to see her, and have to face her; and he knew that she must have told Tom everything. How he had treated her.

He looked at Tom now and he wanted to lie down on the deck and scream for mercy. He wanted to turn and run the other way. His blood seemed to have turned to ice, although he was sweating.

He managed to say: "I will be glad to see her." He did not know how he got the words out, or where he got the strength to move away from the bulkhead and continue walking through the shiny corridors of the ship.

Tom went on: "Remember the first week we were on board ship out of the Academy and you jammed the five-inch gun that almost killed three of the seamen?"

Crossett nodded, but he could not speak. It was like a nightmare, with his past suddenly parading hideously before him.

"Remember," Tom Johnson went on, "how you pleaded to George Reed, who was your room-mate, and told him about how your folks wanted you to be a great naval officer; how you cried and put on one of the acts the movies pay you for doing now, until you convinced George, because he was idealistic and sentimental and noble, and because he had been on the same gun with you and you pointed out how he might have been partly responsible for what happened, that he should shoulder the blame for what happened and clear you? Remember?"

Crossett choked.

"They let George back in the service after the dismissal," Tom Johnson continued, "but of course he could only come in as an enlisted man. It didn't matter, so long as he was in the navy. He—he loved the navy."

"So—he's—back—in?" Crossett managed.

"Yes. He'll be in the wardroom, too. He's a chief petty officer now. Oh yes, and remember how you took Ducky Wilson ashore with you one night and got him drunk? That was when you were dismissed, and Ducky, who had a clear record except for that, had to remain an ensign two years after the rest of us were promoted."

"And—and he's in the wardroom, too?"

Tom Johnson nodded. "Yes. And here the wardroom is." He put his hand on the knob of the door.

Crossett stopped him. His face was livid. "You're crazy if you think I'm going in there. You've tricked me. I'm here to make a picture, not rehash your petty tragedies. You aren't going to get me in there and—and—"

He did not know what he was saying. He was scarcely aware that he lived. He saw Tom jerk his hand away and open the door. He saw the faces of Martha and Ducky and George, and there were more. He had never screamed in his life. But he was a coward, and he screamed now, literally and terribly, choking until his face was blue. He gurgled a jargon of incoherent words about getting off the ship and that he would not stay here. And then he turned and ran. He did not know what he was doing. He wanted only to get away.

2

THAT MESSENGER BOY who worked in a Hollywood Boulevard office of the Western Union was smart, and he would one day be a great columnist, or actor, or cameraman, or movie scout; it was even possible that in his old age he would be a fat producer like Mr. Jonas and smoke cigars. The boy had his eyes open all the time, and he never missed anything. He was a walking news bulletin. He knew when whose option was up and why, if it was not to be renewed. He knew who was going to get married, and vice versa. He even knew who was going to have a baby, and where old stars were and what they were doing. He read Winchell, of course, and Louella Parsons, and listened to Jimmy Fiddler, but these celebrated persons were only the most obvious sources. He had devious ways of digging out information that was never published, or would be published some time in the future. He forecast events for his friends and kept a record of his scoops.

And now that messenger boy was very close to uncovering a fact which only a dozen of the mightiest Hollywood people knew. He walked into a Hollywood Boulevard building and got into the elevator, and then he pulled out a faded column and read the question, the answer of which the columnist himself didn't know.

What well known Hollywood agent is, on the hush, really not an agent at all, but the world's highest paid detective, assigned to solve all studio naughties including murder, and squash unfavorable publicity on the same?

He read that again, and he felt quite sure he was on the right track. He looked at the messages he was to deliver. One was quite plainly an official government communication from the Naval Intelligence; and the other was a cable from Honolulu, the source of the official message. Paramet was shooting "Men of the Fleet" aboard the *Lexington* in Hawaiian waters. What, he reasoned, could be more logical than a crime of some sort occurring on board ship during the making of the film, and the detective who was a movie specialist being called to the scene to help solve it?

He got off the elevator on the fourth floor and walked down the padded hall to a door on which were written in bronze letters:

ANTHONY KEY

Artist's Representative

Motion Pictures.

He entered. He had not been in this office before and he was amazed at the luxury that suddenly surrounded him. A rug into which he sank as deeply as his heels; soft, expensive divan and chair set; a pure teakwood reception table. Directly ahead of him and behind a sliding glass he could see a woman. And she too made the smart Western Union boy catch his breath, for he had seen a lot of beauty in Hollywood, stars and starlets, and he thought he had never seen anyone quite so beautiful as the woman behind the glass. At least one didn't expect to see her sitting at a typewriter.

She was a perfect platinum blonde, and she wore a black patent leather dress which contrasted with her hair, and accentuated the white of her skin, and the size of her soft blue eyes, and the crimson red of her lovely curved lips. The messenger boy had to stop and shake his head. It was as though he had been suddenly transformed into the pleasurable world of a cinema dream.

He saw the glass sliding back now. The girl said: "Those tels for us?"

"Tels?"

"Telegrams," she said, smiling.

He said: "Yeah. You sign right here. One's from the Naval Intelligence." And now he took a chance. "I guess it's another crime for Mr. Key to solve."

The platinum blonde looked up quickly. "What do you mean?"

"Why I—ah, isn't Mr. Key an amateur detective on the side?"

She shook her head. "He certainly is not. Wherever you got that foolish notion get rid of it. When Mr. Key feels he must play, he draws pictures."

The boy gulped. He had known there was a great possibility that he was wrong, but you never got to be a great scoop artist by being afraid to ask questions. He took the signed sheet and left the office. When he got outside he looked at the clipping again, then threw it away in disgust.

"You fake news maker," he muttered.

But he walked to the elevator with a little misgiving, because he still could not understand why the Naval Intelligence would be sending a Hollywood agent official communications.

AS SOON AS the boy left the office Betty Gale got up and hurried back to her boss' office. She had opened the door and was halfway through it when he said:

"Stop!"

She halted as though she had been shot. He went on: "Hold it that way. Chin up a little; that's it, sweetheart. A little frown on your forehead. One foot through the door. Let's see how fast my candid pencil can sketch you."

She held it, because she knew the kind of fits he threw when he wasn't humored, but her scowl increased. She said: "This is great exercise—for you. Maybe it would be easier if I just got Mae West's sculptor to model me in marble. And of course there isn't the faintest possibility that a cable from the romantic islands of atmosphere would be important."

"Nothing so important as beauty in action," he replied, working feverishly with a special leaded pencil. He was a dark man who had smoothly combed hair, and he was very young. He had high cheek bones, and green eyes that reminded one a little of glossy jade. He was clad in a neat blue suit, white shoes, and open polo shirt. A year ago he had been a member of the Federal Bureau of Investigation assigned to Hollywood. But he had retired to devote all of his time to studio and movie location cases. He was paid magnificently from a pool that was taxed from each studio, and the Western Union boy had been right; as an agent he had no clients and sought none. But he had to have an office and since for a number of reasons it seemed advisable that his identity be kept secret he was listed as an artist's representative.

"There," he said at last, "I've got it. How's that, Betty?"

She looked at the sketch, and it wasn't bad considering the speed with which he had done it. She had seen some of his sketches in the newspapers before he quit the F.B.I.; sometimes they had helped find men, and other times they had been used as evidence.

"If the worst ever comes," she told him, "you can always get a job with Walt Disney."

"Thanks," Tony Key replied, "I'll make a note of that. And now to the grimmer aspects of life. Did you say you had something for me; or were you just getting lonesome out there by yourself?"

She laid the telegrams on the mahogany desk in front of him. He glanced up at her, then opened the first one. It was the one from the Naval Intelligence:

KEY—WILLIAM CROSSETT HAS VANISHED PERIOD LAST SEEN IN PASSAGEWAY BELOW DECKS ON LEXINGTON BUT CANNOT BE FOUND PERIOD AS SEVERAL HOURS HAVE PASSED THIS MIGHT BE SERIOUS

BRENNAN

"When Brennan gets excited," Tony Key murmured, "there's no doubt whatever about the seriousness of the case." He opened the cable:

COME AT ONCE ON CHINA CLIPPER STOP CROSSETT HAS DISAPPEARED STOP OUR HALF FILMED PIC IS PARALYZED STOP SUSPECT FOUL PLAY STOP HURRY STOP HAVE YOU ANY IDEAS WHAT MIGHT

HAVE HAPPENED TO THAT SAP BESIDES MURDER
STOP IF SO CABLE THEM.

JOHN JONAS

"It seems," Tony went on, "that Jonas has worked himself up in a lather which must have cost him a lot of dough at the current cable rates."

Betty Gale was reading the cables. "This is all right," she said. "I hope that honey and syrup boy stays hidden until we get there. I've been wanting to leave Holly for the Coral Shores of yonder islands for more months than it would be polite to mention."

"What do you mean: you've been wanting to leave?"

She put her hands on her hips. "Don't tell me I don't get to go along?"

"Did the cable mention you? Besides, who is going to take care of the office?"

She said: "The office will probably rot. What good would it be anyway, without you here? And as for the cable, I'm part and parcel of this business as much as Curly Conley and Max White, your two half-wit strong arm men, am I not?"

"Conley and White are not halfwits. Anyway, you can't go." He got up.

She turned. "Okay. I'll spend the time over at the Columversal lot. I think they have a pic they can—"

"Listen, I'm paying you eighty a week to stay out of pictures. And you wear the diamond engagement ring I gave you. Haven't you *any* respect for me?"

She smiled. "I'm going to phone for *our* China Clipper reservations. Do you want to make a candid pencil sketch of me doing it?"

He resigned himself with a shrug, lighting a cigarette. "Okay, sweetheart." As she went to the phone, he walked over to the window and looked out. He stood there for several minutes listening to her efficiently making all the necessary preparations; and he kept watching Hollywood Boulevard: girls with slacks walking up and down, street cars that moved lazily along their tracks, the two-story buildings of stores, and the sunshine that tumbled across the expansive street.

He had settled down to quiet concentration on how many people might want to kill William Crossett, when a bell ringing brought his attention back to the room. He saw Betty getting up and leaving the office. She returned presently.

"Another cable—and a Western Union boy who keeps insisting you must be a detective."

He did not know why there should be another cable and he was a little excited. They had probably found Crossett's body. He said: "Give me the message. Use your own judgment about the boy."

The slim platinum blonde disappeared again, and Tony Key tore open the envelope. He read it with a great deal of awe for it was from the Intelligence, and more startling than he could have possibly imagined:

KEY—LIEUTENANT-COMMANDER TOM JOHNSON COMMA FRIEND OF CROSSETT COMMA FOUND MURDERED PERIOD WILLIAM CROSSETT STILL MISSING PERIOD IT APPEARS THAT THINGS ABOARD THE LEXINGTON ARE IN SOMEWHAT OF A MESS
BRENNAN

3

IT WAS FOUR in the afternoon, and the ship's bell gonged eight times. The huge gray hulk of the *Lexington* listed lazily to starboard, and churned through the green-blue water in the direction of the tranquil island of Maui. The crowded flight deck was curiously empty of life.

There was confusion in the enlisted compartments. Schedules had been badly disrupted. The movie company aboard had taken no pictures, nor had any seamen seen the great star, Crossett. They did not know what was wrong, and yet a tense and uneasy-cloud hung over the vessel, so that there was not the usual amount of laughter, nor even fights. Sailors sat about looking at magazines, or listening to the radio.

IN THE CONTAGIOUS room of the sick bay Peter Brennan said: "The body doesn't look very nice, does it, Key?"

Peter Brennan of the Naval Intelligence was a tall and very pale young man who had brooding dark eyes, and short clipped black hair. He wore blue uniform trousers, and a leather jacket. A .45 was strapped about his waist.

Tony Key looked at the pajama-clad figure that once had been Tom Johnson. The gray sideburns on the temples were crimson with hard blood, and the firm, rather strong mouth gaped open. The eyes were closed. Key leaned forward and examined the three roundish marks that surrounded the bruises that had broken Johnson's skull.

"No body looks nice," he said. "Brennan, what do you make

of the wounds?"

"They are peculiar. Gun butt or club, I'd say."

Tony Key's green eyes were thoughtful with a faraway look. "Uh-huh. Johnson had his back turned. The killer crept in and let him have it—just as he was buttoning up the top of his pajamas. Right?"

"That's the way I put it together."

Tony looked up. "All right. You ought to know this: would an officer upon retiring to his room, lock the door?"

Peter Brennan's pale face was creased in a faint smile. "Hardly."

"But under the circumstances I mean," Key insisted. "He knows Crossett is missing. Probably around somewhere. Doesn't trust Crossett. Hates him, as you explained. Would he go to bed, leaving his door unlocked?"

Brennan shrugged. "Your guess is as good as mine."

Tony Key said: "My guess is that he wouldn't. So far so good. Is it logical Crossett would know where to find Johnson's room? Since he was in hiding he wouldn't dare ask. If he didn't know where the room was, and he didn't have a key to unlock the door—"

"You mean you don't think Crossett killed him?"

KEY'S EYES FLICKERED. "Definitely not. From what I know of Crossett he hasn't enough courage to kill. I think an enemy of Johnson is taking advantage of the situation. Further: Johnson wasn't killed with a gun butt or club."

"What the hell then was he killed with?"

Key showed his hand. "Now you're going too fast. I don't know." He pulled a pad and pencil from his pocket, glanced again at the curious small round wounds that had broken John-son's skull, and started sketching them.

"We don't know," said Brennan, "and you don't know that Crossett isn't guilty. Personally, I think you're showing off. World's highest paid dick making quick deductions. But it's okay with me. What we want to do is clear this thing up, so if you work your angle, and I work mine, between the two of us we ought to stumble across something hot enough to give us the solution."

Tony Key was still working on the sketch. "Stick to your ideas, Brennan," he said. "Pedal your own bike. But before you shove off, do me a favor and put me up to date on this situation. Anything happened since the murder?"

"Nothing. I've handled everything according to routine. You know that it's regulation to keep a ship at sea when a crime occurs aboard, and that no one is permitted to leave. More: we keep the publicity angle as closed as you and the Hollywood gang try to. So the crew isn't aware of what has happened, although they'll have to be if we don't clean up the mess pretty quickly. We could turn the men to searching for Crossett, for one thing."

"But don't. Not yet. And listen: I'm putting my two trigger finger lads in uniform. How's to let them wander around?" He finished the sketch.

Peter Brennan looked at it over his shoulder.

"Sure. Anything you say, Key. Only I'll have to admit I was kind of floored when I saw you trot that blonde aboard. I didn't expect that you'd bring her."

Tony Key grinned. "Neither did I. But she's here. And maybe it's just as well because she's got a lot of savvy in matters like these. I have her in pumping your suspects in a nice ladylike way. She has more patience than I. Let's go up and see how she's making out. And listen: if I catch you making any passes at her, I'll do my damndest to hang the murder around *your neck.*"

They left the contagious ward, and Brennan locked the door. They started down the corridor at a fast pace.

When they arrived in the wardroom, Betty Gale was sitting in one corner with her arms crossed. Her notebook lay thrown across the table. Martha Johnson was crying, and the officers in the room seemed bleak and unsympathetic.

"Hello, boss!" said Betty. "I've got a present for you."

Tony Key said: "Swell."

He glanced back as John Jonas waddled into the room and sat down. The fat producer seemed very nervous; the cigar in his mouth was out, though he did not appear to be aware of it. Lieutenant George Reed and Junior-Lieutenant Ducky Wilson looked at him significantly, then over at Martha Johnson.

Reed appeared to be perfectly confident of both himself and the situation, but Ducky Wilson, red haired and pale, was keenly observant, and in spite of his flip rejoinders, gave clue to his nervousness by his mannerisms: tugging at his collar, as though he suffocated; rubbing the back of his fingers, which seemed grayish and not exactly clean. Tony noticed that Betty seemed to like Ducky; he observed this not a little jealously. But if she were prejudiced in Wilson's favor, she made up for it in her obvious dislike for the cold and distant George Reed. Reed was frigid. You would have thought he had slept all night between two pieces of ice.

Key sat down beside the naval officer's dark wife.

SHE WAS SLIM, and dynamic, and very pretty. Her hair was a rich and shining black, coiled on the back of her neck; the beauty of her face was pale and exotic, with a kittenish slant to her eyes, and a thin nose, the nostrils of which were wide. Her lips were a flare of red. Key had met her once as Crossett's wife. It was at a premiere at Grauman's Chinese, and she had looked stunning. For the rest he had picked up gossip about her from Hollywood's wise boys who were always in the know of such things.

She had a Latin temper; hot blood that needed a constant stimulant of excitement. No one knew how much Latin there was in her, however, they only knew she was inclined to be dramatic, and extreme to the point of being unbearable in everything she did. It had not been a secret that Crossett treated her badly, for more than once she had worn smoked glasses on the boulevard to cover a black eye, but here again the Latin seemed to answer the question of why she stayed with him; for although such women will scream for freedom and equal rights, Key thought, it is tradition with them to be bossed by the male, to have ironclad law laid down to them; and in their secret heart they admire a man who will do this, even if he is ruthless, more than they do one who will let them have their own way. Until the day she disappeared from Crossett's household everyone had believed she worshipped him.

She looked at Key now. "It is terrible," she said, and she daubed at her eyes. "But I must be brave."

Betty Gale was grinning. Tony Key looked at her.

"The present I have," Betty said, "is in that notebook. Only it happens to be in shorthand, which you wouldn't understand. Shall I whisper it?"

Peter Brennan said: "What is this—a game?"

The platinum blonde nodded toward Martha. "She has confessed the murder."

There was silence. Martha Johnson kept crying softly.

"But that's not the complete payoff," Betty Gale went on. "William Crossett is—Mr. Jonas will be glad to hear—alive. Living and breathing, just as you and I. He's hiding in the empty stateroom Mrs. Johnson was given to sleep in last night."

4

TONY KEY LOOKED at Peter Brennan. Neither of them spoke. Jonas and the two officers, Wilson and Reed, seemed not in the least surprised. Brennan started moving toward the door. There was still silence, and Tony Key could feel the gentle list of the huge ship. At last Martha Johnson leapt to her feet.

"Well, gentlemen? What are you going to do? I killed my husband. I had reason. He was going to murder poor Bill Crossett. There was only one way I could stop him from doing it. So I—" She sank down in the chair again.

Key said: "Look, Betty, you show her some card tricks or something to keep her interested. If she thinks she killed Johnson humor her along. I see that you already have. Brennan and I are—"

"You mean you don't believe it?" Betty snapped.

"Oh sure, we believe it," Key answered, "only we are very methodical detectives and we like to hear everyone make his little speech. We like to have reasons for things, and logic." He was backing.

"So, as I say, keep the folks amused until we come back. You might get up and recite the Shooting of Dan McGrew; that always goes over big. Or try standing on your head. No, on second thought, you'd better not. Just recite. We'll be right back."

He slipped out into the corridor and caught up with Peter Brennan.

"She might have done it, Key," he said.

"Sure she might have," Tony agreed, "but in the event she hasn't why encourage the killer by making him think we're giving up the chase? The trail will turn into a piece of ice if he thinks he's in the clear. He'll shut his trap and let us railroad the pretty Latin."

"Yeah. I see your point. Personally, I'm much more interested in play-games. Such as third degree, with Bill Crossett."

"Strange, but I had the same thought," said Key. "You know where this room is, don't you?"

"Sure."

In the next moment they had stopped in front of the door. Brennan turned the knob, grunted: "Locked," and brought out a string of keys. The third one he tried clicked back the lock. Tony Key reached inside his coat to the shoulder holster that carried his Colt automatic. He had a strange premonition.

Brennan pushed the door open, and for a moment Key and the Intelligence Officer stood in the passageway and looked in. The room seemed empty, bleak. Brennan stepped in first, and Tony Key followed.

Almost immediately, shots roared from behind. Peter Brennan went down as he tried to turn about. Tony Key saw the strained look on his face. But he saw it for only a fraction of a second. For he, too, was turning, but both he and Brennan had been taken off guard and he was not quick enough. Another shot roared.

Key felt pain sear across the tip of his shoulder, and though the bullet did no more than furrow him, he went careening across the room. He crashed against the bulkhead, and thudded down into a sitting position. He had struggled to keep his mind clear, and even as he hit he was raising the automatic in his hand.

IT JUMPED AS he pulled the trigger, and for the first time now he saw the face of the man before him. It was a face livid with fear, yet unmistakable: William Crossett. The dark eyes were blazing. Tony Key triggered the automatic a second time. He saw Crossett's body jerk and quiver against the bulkhead. He saw the actor grasp his side. A scream broke from his lips, but died in a choking that came from his throat. He started going down, his feet sliding out from under him. And yet he was desperate enough to hold the gun steady in his hand. Another bullet blasted from its muzzle.

Key heard the metal slug clang into the iron bulkhead an inch over his ear; and he returned fire, two rapid shots. He missed because Crossett suddenly fell quickly across the floor of the stateroom. For a moment he lay still and Key watched him. At last the Hollywood detective grabbed the corner of the bed and hauled himself to his feet.

He saw Peter Brennan holding his stomach and writhing in pain. Crossett stirred. Tony Key drew a slim pair of handcuffs from his coat pocket and bent over the actor. He grabbed his hand.

But in the next moment he was being jerked off his feet. Crossett had been acting again; and now he was a living fury. He grabbed Key's arm, jerked him headlong over his body; and as Key fell, slid out from under him. Tony Key struggled to get to his feet. He saw Crossett standing again, saw the gun in his hand.

He dove at the weapon, but Crossett lifted it, and bashed the butt into Key's forehead. For a moment Tony could not see and he staggered back. The gun butt hit again. Crossett laughed as though he had lost his mind. Tony Key groped out blindly.

He heard the door slam and stumbled toward it. His vision was clearing now, but his head was throbbing, and blood was running from the top of his skull down into his eyes.

He opened the door and plunged out into the corridor. He reached in for the gun he had put away when he started to handcuff Crossett. The weapon slid into his hand, but as he looked to take aim, he saw a blurred vision before his eyes. There seemed to be not one fleeting figure, but three.

And then—quite suddenly—everything was clear. He saw Crossett trying to run, and still holding his shoulder. Tony Key moved forward; he lifted his gun and aimed at the shoulder. The weapon jerked in his hand. But the bullet clanged into an overhead beam ahead of Crossett, and now the actor had rounded a corner. Tony Key, his mind standing on the brink of blackness, started running. A cry broke from his lips.

In the next moment his legs gave out, and he pitched forward on his bleeding head. The bullet wound, and the slugging he had taken, had weakened him. He lay writhing on deck, cursing; he told himself he had to get up and keep going. But his muscles would not respond.

PLATINUM BETTY GALE carefully washed his head with a warm cloth that felt like something just short of paradise. He was in the sick bay, and Peter Brennan lay in the bunk just opposite Tony's chair.

"As for me," said Betty, "I'll take Charlie Chan any old time. Or a nice six-reel program pic where a flatfoot named Kelly rescues his daughter by jumping through the rafters onto a table, where the six gangsters are playing stud poker to see which one is going to kiss the little gal. Kelly kicks three of them in the face, and shoots the other three. It looks very simple. There's nothing to it. But what do you super men do? The two of you let a weakling actor put you in the sickbay of a ship."

Tony Key grinned.

"It's not funny," she went on, "when the world's most conceited detective, who charges more for his time than Jean Harlow, falls for the old gag of someone hiding behind the door as it is opened."

"I tell you it wasn't the door. It was a closet on the other side of the door, that you don't see as you enter because it's right smack up against the bulkhead. He waited until we were in, had our backs turned, and then he jumped out and let us have it. Hell—any guy can—"

"Yeah, I know. Explain that to the moguls on next pay day. And just *try* and keep your job if you press charges against Crossett for this—if he doesn't happen to be guilty of the Johnson murder. Remember, he's still the box office syrup that little girls go to bed and ask Providence to send them, and remember—"

"I tell you he's lost his mind!" Tony Key said.

"What? Because he shot you? Don't be silly. I've felt like doing it myself. By the way, if you are interested, Martha Johnson still sticks to her confession, and Miss Betty Gale, your blonde admirer, still thinks she is guilty."

"That's the cat in you, Betty. Trying to frame a beautiful woman."

"What do you mean: trying to frame?"

He put a cigarette in his mouth and lit it. "Did it occur to you to ask her what kind of a weapon she used?"

"No. And hold still while I get this last bandage tied."

Key glanced over at Brennan. "How you feeling?"

"Rotten."

"Think you'll live?"

But Peter Brennan was too sick to appraise humor. He closed his eyes. Tony Key got to his feet.

"Hop back to the wardroom, Betty. Get some officer to gather our guests again; I'll want to see them. I'm back to just where I was before: trying to get a lead on Johnson's murder. But since Crossett prefers to stick around the officer's rooms, and since Martha is undoubtedly giving him all the help she can, I have an idea where he might be. It's worth a check at least."

"Okay. I'll see you in the wardroom."

THE SHIP'S BELL gonged six times. It was seven o'clock, and the *Lexington* moved silently through the calm night sea, in line now with the rest of the fleet; huge red and green running lights glowed from the port and starboard side; the planes lay quiet and alone on the flight deck. The tiny lights of Maui glimmered faintly far off shore.

Tony Key moved through the lighted passageway to the room in which Tom Johnson had been murdered. It had come to him while he was being bandaged that this room, being around the corner from where Tony had fallen, might easily be used as a hideout. The murder room had to be undisturbed because of any clues that might be in it and would have to be used later to prove the crime against somebody.

But it was only a hunch, coupled with the logic that Crossett was not likely to take his chances running around a ship he did not know much about. He was so famous that any sailor would be able to spot him. The ironic twist to it was that since the ship was unaware of the murder, Crossett could have walked any deck he wanted and the sailors, aware that he was aboard, would have thought it was perfectly natural for him to look around, and would not have bothered him. But maybe Crossett did know this. Tony decided that if he did not find him in the stateroom, he would have Crossett's disappearance announced through the loudspeakers with a request that when found he be brought to the wardroom. He was tired of hide and seek and although he had honestly believed Crossett innocent of Tom Johnson's murder, he was now by no means so sure, and he wanted to get Crossett's whole story.

He attributed Martha Johnson's confession to hysteria, and yet it brought home a curious fact of which no one had been aware: she still loved to the point of worship—William Crossett.

He arrived at the stateroom door and glanced up at the card: *Lieutenant-Commander Thomas Johnson.* He thought of Johnson lying in the contagious ward. He tried the door. It was open!

It should have been locked. He reached for his gun, and, green eyes curiously hard, he shoved open the door. He slipped into the room, keeping his back to the bulkhead this time and looking first behind the door, and toward the nearest closets. But he could see little through the light from the passageway, and he snapped on the switch in the room. A figure lay in the bed, cover over him. It was Crossett.

Key walked over to him. He felt the ship sway gently to the starboard. A green wave broke over the closed port hole and water dribbled down. He kept looking down at Crossett. The actor did not move, and Tony Key felt his face. Suddenly he drew his hand away and pushed back a pillow which covered the top of Crossett's head. The pillow gave hard, for blood glued it to Crossett's hair.

Crossett was murdered.

The silence in the room was ominous. Water kept dribbling down the port hole. The ship creaked a little as it swayed. Tony Key put his gun away and bent over the corpse. He saw two small, roundish marks on the skull. The same kind of wounds he had seen on Johnson.

He pulled back the covers. There was the bullet wound that he himself had put in Crossett's side, and there was much blood around it. One of Crossett's hands was still pressed over the side.

Tony Key thought the air in the room was close, and somehow damp—almost soggy. He lit a cigarette and moved away from the body. He stepped out into the passageway and quietly closed the door.

5

MARTHA JOHNSON SAID: "While Bill was on location, Tom Johnson came to see me every day. He was on leave. He said he knew, everybody knew, how Bill treated me. He made me think I was in love with him again, and that we could make a go of it. So he took me away, and I got a quick divorce from Bill. But I was always sorry for it. I loved Bill Crossett."

"So you thought he had murdered Tom Johnson and you were trying to be noble by taking the rap for him?"

"Yes. You see Tom knew how I felt about Bill Crossett and he said we were going to have it out in this wardroom when Bill came aboard. But Bill never came in the wardroom. When he found my room later, he told me Tom had threatened to kill him. He was in a terrible condition. He was out of his mind."

"What time was this?"

"About four in the morning. He said he had run into the first room he came to, to hide, and it happened to be Tom's room. He heard Tom Johnson tell an officer what room to take me to, and then he stayed hidden and Tom did not find him. He said he didn't remember much of what happened in the hours that followed, but that when he came out of the closet the door of which had been tightly closed, Tom was on the floor dead."

"But you thought in his dilemma he—Crossett—had killed Tom and was just telling you that?"

"Yes. Naturally, having heard where I was, he came to me. He thought then that I hated him, but he didn't know where else to go and—and he had always been able to bluff me. He thought he would bluff me again. But he didn't have to."

Tony Key nodded. It was very simple. "And when he left your room after our little battle, he went back to the only stateroom he knew—Tom Johnson's."

"I—I guess he did."

Key pinched out his cigarette. His green eyes were hot. "Look Mrs. Johnson. Think hard! Didn't someone else know of Crossett's whereabouts? Didn't someone else offer to help him?"

"I don't know. He didn't mention anybody."

"Think hard. It is quite important. Because that *somebody* whom he thought had befriended him, is more than likely the person who murdered him."

She repeated: "He didn't mention anyone. But as I said, he was out of his mind. He talked wildly."

Tony Key looked up at Lieutenant George Reed, then at Junior-Lieutenant Ducky Wilson.

"You two gentlemen," he said quickly, "you have been very patient, but it won't be necessary any longer. We are getting to you right now. You see, this thing has narrowed itself down beautifully. We look for motive in murders and the party responsible for the two that have happened aboard this ship must have a motive that includes both an officer and an actor. Since you two were the only ones familiar with Johnson and Crossett; that is, could have reason for wanting either one of them killed, it puts you on somewhat of a spot. Which of you wishes to confess first?"

REED SPOKE FIRST. He was tall and blonde, definitely Nordic. He had suspicious blue eyes, and his expression was one of highbrow tolerance with proceedings that did not greatly interest him. He seemed no more moved than he had during Martha's confession a little earlier.

Key did not particularly like him because he was so prim and dandy, with his immaculate appearance and his lack of emotion. Apparently murder did not even annoy him. He was as unlike Ducky Wilson—whom to Key's regret Betty Gale still smiled upon—as sun and moon.

Wilson was untidy. As time passed he seemed to become less interested in personal appearance: since dinner he seemed to have spotted the cuff of his coat with grease but he was totally unaware; or he just didn't give a damn. His hair cut seemed to have suddenly grown shaggy because he was unkempt.

But now Reed was talking and Tony had to pay attention to him. Reed, his fingernails carefully manicured; his face beautifully groomed; sitting, playing with a watch chain and talking. He was saying:

"I had no feeling of friendliness for Crossett. He caused me to resign the navy for an accident on a five-inch gun for which he was responsible. But that was my own fault. I was young and idealistic. I thought at that time that he was worth taking the blame for. Johnson told Crossett I was now a chief petty officer, and that day when he was to bring Crossett in, he asked me to wear a chief's uniform. Johnson was my friend, so I humored him. But the fact is that when Crossett finally went out of the navy he wrote out a confession of the gun incident, explaining the entire circumstances, and that, with a petition of the ship on which I had served, brought about my reinstatement in the service as an officer."

"The idea being," Tony Key said, "that Mr. Johnson was deliberately trying to scare the daylights out of Crossett and took advantage of his not knowing you had been reappointed."

"That seems to be the idea."

"I see. And you felt no malice toward Crossett?"

"None whatsoever. As a matter of fact I was rather thankful he wrote the confession." The blonde officer's blue eyes flickered.

Tony Key looked at him for a moment, then he swung toward Ducky Wilson. Wilson had red hair and bright black eyes. He was thin, and pale; but he had a strong jaw.

"Me," he said, "I hated Crossett like hell, and I don't mind telling you."

"You were the man who got drunk with him?"

"Yes."

Tony's right eyebrow arched. "But you didn't kill him, of course. You wouldn't do anything like that?"

"You're right," said Ducky Wilson cheerfully, putting a cigarette in his mouth and lighting it, "I wouldn't."

Tony Key did not reply, and for a long moment there was silence. Betty Gale tossed her notebook to the table and exercised her fingers back and forth.

"At this point, boss," she said, "in keeping with the best pic policies, Charlie Chan would put an empty gun on the table and let the killer grab for it. Or was that Nero Wolfe?"

John Jonas, the fat producer, who had said nothing for a long while, grunted and touched a match to his cigar. "I wish you'd do something, Key. The picture is lost without Crossett. I might as well get back to Hollywood."

Tony Key took in the flabby face of the producer curiously. He looked into the beady eyes that seemed to be lost in mountains of flesh. "You aren't married, are you, Mr. Jonas?"

"No."

"But you were thinking of it?"

"No."

"Yes, you were thinking of it. Nice new starlet. Young and ambitious. But she met Crossett."

"You're making this up. Are you going to try and accuse me? I'm one of your employers!"

Tony Key was restless. He walked from one end of the room to the other. Presently he swung around, shot his finger out.

"No. I'm not accusing you, Mr. Jonas. I'm not accusing anyone. I don't have to. Inside of an hour I'll *know* without a bit of doubt who committed these crimes. Whoever did it will be locked up. You see, Mr. Peter Brennan of the Naval Intelligence picked up a clue from Johnson's body that had to be analyzed—set in a chemical for a great many hours. But it's almost ready now, and that clue combined with another Brennan has, will pin the crime definitely on the right party!"

JONAS SUCKED IN his breath. Lieutenant Reed's blue eyes seemed suddenly troubled, the first emotion he had registered since Key had been watching him. Red-haired Ducky Wilson shifted uneasily. Martha Johnson stared, wide-eyed.

"And so," Tony Key went on, "until we are ready, I believe you people may as well go back to your rooms. I want to shake each of you by the hand and wish you my best, because the next time we meet, well—"

Lieutenant George Reed said: "Isn't this just a bit ridiculous?"

"It won't seem that way an hour from now. There were just certain things I had to learn from you people, and I think I know as much as I need to know. Mainly, motives. Miss Gale has the written testimony witnessed by all of you. The testimony of one of you will be used for a conviction of murder in the first degree. That is all."

Jonas got up and went to the door. Tony Key shook his hand. Reed and Ducky Wilson followed. He shook hands with both of them. Martha Johnson departed last.

Key closed the door, and wiped sweat from his forehead.

Platinum Betty Gale said: "Well, I see you took the hint and laid the gun on the table. What's the plan?"

He put his handkerchief in his pocket. "Betty, was it convincing?"

"You mean the clue that's pickling in vinegar? It's marvelous. Where did you get it?"

"Out of the air. But I think the murderer fell for it. I'm sure of it. Now, look: we've got to work fast. Curly Conley and Max White are wandering around the ship somewhere in sailor uniforms. Get them. Send White here with the make-up kit at once, and send Conley down to guard Brennan. He must guard him with his life. Brennan's a sick man, and I don't want anybody fooling with him."

"Oke. But I still don't know what the plan is."

"Do you have to know everything?"

She shrugged. "I just happened to think if you were killed there would be no one to know what course of action your genius had decided to take."

"If I'm killed there'll be no one to care, because the murderer will be caught killing me."

She had started for the door, but now she turned. "Boss, you mean to say—"

He grinned and showed her his hand. "Go ahead on your

errand, hardhearted; until you got so nasty I was going to tell you who the killer is. But—"

"You mean you know?"

"Yes, I know."

She was incredulous. "You're absolutely positive?"

"Absolutely."

"Then why don't you—"

"Because the clue I got might not be strong enough to hang the guilty-party; but the new scheme, if it works, will bring the killer right into our hands."

Betty Gale said: "What clue are you talking about?"

"The clue I got when I shook hands with them," Tony Key replied.

THE SHIP'S BELL gonged four times. It was ten o'clock and the *Lexington* was following the *Saratoga* and *Ranger* and drawing near the dark tropic island of Molokai; the lights of portholes were out now, and marines walked guard on the flight deck. The black, silken water rippled and gurgled against the side of the monster vessel as it nosed into the silver light of the moon.

Taps had blown and the enlisted men who were not on watch were in their bunks. But even a whisper can become a scream that has no sound, and there was very little sleeping. Low toned voices echoed.

"Hey, Butch. I was on watch. You know what I heard?"

"What?"

"Crossett's been murdered."

"You said that before. I still don't believe you."

"Yeah, well get a load of this: Commander Johnson's been murdered too."

"What do you mean?"

"Just what I said, Butch. I heard that both Crossett and Johnson have been murdered."

"That's scuttlebutt talk."

"No. I got it from the bridge. Heard a chief quartermaster telling a signalman."

"Did the chief know for sure?"

"Well, no, he didn't. Not exactly. But if you ask me, Butch—"

"I'm not asking you. For cripes' sake go to bed."

6

ONLY A BLUE stanchion light shone from one corner of the sick bay, and in its eerie glow a figure was silhouetted on a white cot. A figure who lay there alone, unmoving. The ship swayed to starboard and bottles rattled from the shelves, but there was no other sound.

Presently there was another figure. One who opened the door and peered in. A flashlight gleamed across the bunks, and at last rested on the one in which a man lay. The figure crossed the room silently. He put the light down on the face. Then he turned it off.

"Brennan!" he whispered.

"Yes?"

"What happened to your clue?"

The man in the bunk blinked. "Clue?—Oh. It isn't ready yet. Will be pretty quickly."

"Where is it?"

The man on the bunk said: "I haven't told anyone where it is. Why should I tell you?"

"You haven't even told Tony Key?"

"No. Of course not."

The man with the flashlight laughed softly. "And you aren't going to tell anyone."

He put the light away and lifted his fist. Tony Key rose from the bed, grabbed at that fist, and cried out. The lights went on. Key threw the killer across the bed, and to the floor. He tumbled out on top of him. Curly Conley rushed from his hiding place, a gun in hand; Max White, also armed, stood guarding the door. Betty Gale watched from a corner of the room.

The killer struggled desperately. He struck out at Key, but the Hollywood detective was pinning down his arms. Suddenly the murderer's legs swept up, got a grip on Key's shoulders and started tugging back. The place where Tony had been wounded was ripped open and began bleeding. The shoulder felt numb.

Conley and White could not shoot or intrude without harm to their boss either physically, or by getting awkwardly in the way. It was a breathless moment in which everything depended on Tony Key's ability to extricate himself.

Key was swung back by the grip of the other on his shoulders. He felt the killer writhing free, and crawling back. He rolled, saw an upraised arm, a glitter of brass. The blow fell for his head, but Key ducked so that it missed by an inch, hitting him just below the base of his neck. It had come within a fraction of hitting his spinal column.

He saw the fist raise again, but he swung his own right, crashed it into the murderer's face. Reaching behind him and grabbing the bunk, he pulled himself to his feet. The killer started to rise also. In that split second, almost on his feet, Tony Key brought up his knee with all the impact he could force behind it. It thudded under the killer's jaw.

The murderer fell back, groggy. Tony Key moved across to the other side of the bed and Curly Conley and Max White moved forward and picked the man up. In a moment he was wearing handcuffs.

Betty Gale wet the end of her pencil. "Any little statement you'd like to make at this point, Mr. Wilson? Or should I call you Junior-Lieutenant Ducky Wilson?"

THE RED-HAIRED OFFICER stared at her, and gulped. Sweat was drenching his face. His black eyes were livid. He looked from Betty to Tony Key who was removing the thin mask that make-up expert Max White had moulded from Brennan's face. He blinked as though he could not comprehend.

"Then you weren't Brennan?"

"No. Unfortunately Brennan was too sick to play the part."

"Part?"

"Yeah," said Betty Gale, "you know: gun on the table, and you reach for it. Same thing. You stuck your neck out."

"Mainly because I needed those brass knucks to convict you with," Tony Key added. "I was afraid when I saw the tarnish where you wore them across your hands—the tarnish and the creases and marks they left—that if I arrested you there in the wardroom we'd never find the knucks. So I invited you to come down here. There was no clue, except that one. I knew from the beginning that it hadn't been a gun or a club that had bashed in Johnson's head. I've taken sketches of heads that were like that, and the sketch I made of Johnson's head wasn't the same. The marks where you cracked the skull were too round, not blunt enough. And they were too small.

"But that isn't all," Tony Key went on smoothly. "You were a give-away almost since the beginning." He glanced at Betty, arching his right eyebrow. "A point you seemed to have missed, my pretty; you were all giggles and blushes over Wilson."

"That's not true, papa," she said. "I had a hunch from the beginning that he was the bogy man, and I treated him nice so he wouldn't take a swack at me. I think I smell what you're coming to; let's see if my reasons for suspecting him coincide with yours. Almost from the beginning, he was trying to rub the grayish tarnish off his paws. It looked like he had dirty hands. But the tarnish came from the old brass knucks. Second, after he bumped Crossett he didn't have time to dandy up and he looked—if you will pardon my Southern accent—like hell. Hair not combed, shirt dirty, collar open. Yeah—and the spot on his coat that looked like grease because he had washed it. It was blood, wasn't it?"

"Betty," Tony sighed, "you're marvelous!"

She said: "You will be too, if you keep me long enough."

Key sobered and looked around. "Savvy now?"

The handcuffed officer looked down at the brass knuckles on his hands with which he had just tried to kill Tony Key.

"Uh-huh," he breathed, "I get your idea all right."

"And then," Key went on, "motive helped point you too. You should have let Crossett live. When you saw him dash into Johnson's room after the shooting, you should have just left him there. In time, if he didn't call for help, he would have bled to death of the bullet wound in his side. And he wouldn't have called for help because his fright, and the added weight of Johnson's murder, had unbalanced his mind, temporarily at least. As I say, you should have left him, but you didn't. You went and killed him. You should know better, Wilson."

"Know better than what?"

"Than to take a woman of Latin temperament seriously under such circumstances. After Martha had been married to Johnson again for a while, she knew she didn't love him, and although it was not possible by that time to go back to Crossett, she was by no means going to suffer in silence. She was hot-blooded and romantic. She must have dazzled you awfully.

Oh, I know you probably had some small personal motive—probably jealousy—for killing Johnson; and that you had another motive for Crossett, which was that he was responsible for you still being a JG—I know that, but your main motive was to get them out of the way. You wanted Martha for yourself. That's why you killed them."

"You're only guessing that I love her!"

"No, I'm not guessing. It's the only sane motive you could have for being so eager to get Crossett out of the way. You realized too late that she loved him, so you were intent on doing him in. But your error was in mistaking Martha's loneliness and affection for love."

Ducky Wilson looked down, still rubbing at the tarnish. "Yes," he said, "fatal error."

Murder at Eight

Detective Tony Key argues with a stutter gun

IF SONNY LLOYD, of Western Union's Hollywood Boulevard office, hadn't been a messenger boy, he'd have made a great dirt columnist. He had a cunning genius for discovering the most guarded secrets of about three-quarters of the cinema center's biggest celebrities. He should have been whipping up some gossip in competition with Walter Winchell and Jimmie Fiddler instead of pedaling his bike down Vine Street. Vine was winding, and smooth and he could go like hell. The kid wove in and out through swank cars, taxicabs, and Fords.

Suddenly he veered to the right, and jerked up on the handle bars, neatly jumping the curb, and wheeling across a beautiful plot of freshly grown lawn. He hopped off the bike while it was still in motion and scrambled up the marble steps to the porch. He leaned against the door bell, forgetting to let it up for breath. With his other hand he took off his cap, lifting a telegram out of it with his mouth. It was the first of four other telegrams in his cap.

The door was jerked open and an angry little man who had black hair slicked back on his head screamed angrily:

"What the hell do you think you're doing? Get your finger off that bell!"

"Yes, sir," said Sonny. "Telegram."

"So what?"

"So sign for it," Sonny told him. "You're the human rabbit, ain't you?"

"Human rabbit!" the man whispered hoarsely, and though he

was no taller than Sonny, he started getting big, of a sudden. His chest swelled. The white sauce dish that was his face turned an ugly red and his jet black eyes narrowed. He jammed his hands into the pockets of his red smoking jacket. "Young man," he began, "do you know—"

"I know Hollywood," said the boy, "that's why they picked

me to deliver this message when it came in. As a matter of fact, there's an office closer than mine."

"What do you mean?"

"I mean I knew that the human rabbit was Mart Brown, the stunt king."

"Only my enemies call me a rabbit," said Mart Brown. "Do you mean to say that telegram addresses me like that? No name? No address?"

"Right," Sonny told him, "and, for the love of cripes, take it, I'm getting tired holding it."

The Human Rabbit signed for the message and Sonny, with a backward glance, ran down the steps and mounted his bike. In another minute he was whirling off the curbing, and headed toward Sunset Boulevard.

He stopped in front of a good looking stucco house just the other side of Highland. He jumped the steps three at a time, taking the second of the four telegrams from his hat.

A servant answered the door and Sonny said, "I've got to see George McGeorge personally. That's my order on these deliveries."

"But Mr. McGeorge is creating."

"What?" asked Sonny.

"I said, Mr. McGeorge is writing a story. He works at home instead of the studio. Quieter."

"I see," said Sonny, and started leaning on the bell again.

"Here! You can't do that!"

"It won't be quiet until he comes and signs for this telegram," Sonny murmured. He began to whistle.

George McGeorge was there in another minute. He was a tallish man who had dark, wavy hair. He looked more like an actor than a writer.

"Where do I sign?" McGeorge asked softly.

"Right here," said Sonny.

A few minutes later he was riding the bike up one of the hills that headed into Hollywoodland. It was a tough jaunt but he made it easier by thinking that coming back he could coast all the way. He arrived in front of a white cottage around which grew flowers and vines. He had no trouble with servants. Marian Cox answered the door herself.

She was very pretty, and very young. Sonny confused the issue as much as possible so she would take a long time signing the slip and he watched her with a vague yearning in his heart.

Marian Cox wasn't twenty yet, though she had already starred in two good pictures. Her hair was a soft brown, and her eyes like violets. Her skin was so white and so fragile that he thought if he touched it, it would break. She was tiny, and delicate, and graceful, yet the most dynamic thing about her was a sweetness in her personality. Not too sweet. You knew she had been kissed; and you knew she wasn't a prude. It was a manner that, affected or not, put her in a class by herself, even among stars.

"Thank you," she said, as she took the telegram. She put a half dollar in his hand.

"Thank *you*, Miss Cox," said Sonny.

He got his bike and started coasting in the general direction of Hollywood Boulevard. He had already forgotten Marian Cox because he was thinking of something else: the telegrams. He had been given three to deliver, but he was on his way with a fourth one. He had written this one on the teletype himself and addressed it to Anthony Key.

Though it was against the laws of the company, Sonny had

read the three telegrams. They all said the same thing. He had sensed the drama in them, and the thought of what was to follow chilled his blood; and since it was his own personal idea that Tony Key was a detective, Sonny had made an additional copy of the message for Key. Of course, Hollywood (with the possible exception of a chosen few producers and the local police) believed Key to be what he was listed: a moving-picture agent. But because he had delivered telegrams to Key, and because Sonny was, if nothing else, an observing young man, he had reached the conclusion that the agency was a blind; that Tony Key was assigned to all studio crimes, not only to solve them, but to keep the publicity of the unpleasant ones out of the paper. He was (if Sonny was right about his being a detective) paid a big salary. A salary that would give Tony Key the rightful title of the world's highest paid investigator.

Too, Sonny Lloyd knew (who didn't?) that Barton Boyce, a handsome but broke has-been of the silent days, had been missing for three days. The very thing that prevented Boyce from being in talkies had kept him in the public eye. The dashing, gallant flicker hero of a happier era was tongue tied. A studio had put him in a picture and let someone else talk his dialogue, the blow-off coming when, on the night of the premiere, a columnist broadcast the news from Coast to Coast. It killed the picture, but it was so funny, and so typically Hollywood that both the reporter who had dished the scoop and the unfortunate tongue-tied Barton Boyce had remained, in a news sense, in the lap of the public ever since.

So when Boyce was reported missing it made the headlines, and ever since there had been a front page story about the fact that he was still gone. Sonny Lloyd thought it likely that Key was working on that case right now. This knowledge, along with his unconfirmed suspicion that Tony Key was the world's highest paid detective, had prompted Sonny to write out the additional message. His motive was, that if Key *did* work on the case, that was proof he was a detective, and Sonny would have another brilliant deduction to mark in his honor column in the little black book he kept for such purposes.

The message that had gone to Mart Brown (the Human Rabbit), George McGeorge, Marian Cox, and was now on its way to Tony Key, read as follows:

> *Barton Boyce issues you an exclusive invitation to the most spectac-ular performance of his career stop tonight at eight stop stand outside the white circle that will be marked on sidewalk on corner of Wilshire and LaBrea stop important that you come alone*

MARIAN COX SAT in the chair and just stared at the telegram. The curious sensation that had come over her when she had first read it was gone and in its place something in her chest felt hard, like iron, so that it was difficult for her heart to keep beating. She was afraid because she knew Barton Boyce and she knew he had neither written the telegram nor autho-rized it to be sent. Probably no one could be more sure of this than she.

She sat there, cold and numb, as though it were impossible for her to move. She thought of her work in stock, and her rise to fame (through the help of George McGeorge) and how cheerful Barton Boyce had been, never jealous, always enthusiastic when something better came. She thought of the Sundays she had spent at his cottage in Malibu where they had made miniature movies of themselves, from scripts they wrote together and had friends film.

"At least," Barton had laughed, "I can be a star on your screen at home."

Yet Barton had not told her he wanted to make her his wife because he felt he possessed too little to ask, and as she thought of this, tears wanted to come to her eyes, but she had cried so many times since Barton disappeared that there were no tears left, and she sat there, the telegram in her lap. She was thinking that the words "spectacular" and "performance" and "invitation" did not smack of Barton.

She got up from the chair and went to the telephone. She looked at it, and she thought it was strange that this awful suspense about someone should come into her life. Before, there had only been songs and happiness, and a burning, seething ambition to become a good actress.

She took the telephone and put her hand on the cold receiver. She had been ready to dial the police, but at the last moment she dialed another number. She did not know why she did this. She called the home of George McGeorge.

George McGeorge was one of the fastest writers in the business, and despite the fact that during his heyday in magazines he had twice copped O'Henry awards, one might have called him a hack, except that no hack in the world could make two thousand dollars a week. And that was exactly what he made.

Just before his phone rang he had put the telegram down beside the pages of his new scenario and stared at it. He was trying to clock his feelings. He always did this. Even when he went to the funeral of a good friend he spent more time analyzing how he felt than he did thinking of the dead man. He had been writing emotions for years and he thought it was strange he scarcely ever really felt any himself. He was known as a great follower of fact and the first thing he thought of was that this would make a swell picture. Of course he would have to see the conclusion, but he would not necessarily have to write it that way. He smiled a little coldly. Barton Boyce had been a good guy, but what the hell!

Boyce had been in his way, hadn't he?

He lit a cigarette, and read the telegram over again. Then the phone rang. He sat down as he answered.

"Hello, Marian."

"George," she said, "I got a telegram about Barton." She read it to him.

"I got one, too," he said.

"What can it mean?"

"I don't know." At this point, he thought, a scenario would say: "Play it up. Barton was your friend. You are concerned. A vital message has just come."

"I don't know," he repeated. "But we'll find out tonight. Don't worry, sweetheart, Bart will be all right. I sort of hunch those things, you know. Feel them."

"We must call the police," said she.

He thought that this would not be right. "No," he told her, "the telegram said to come alone. That may be important. If it's a kidnaping, for instance, the cops would scare Bart's deliverers away. No, not the police."

And he went on like that.

MART BROWN (THE Human Rabbit) had the ability of being able to work himself up into a lather very easily. And now he was in a lather and he had not even had to work to get it. He paced up and down in his half-dark living-room with the telegram in his hand. He thought of many things, and at last, determined, he went to the telephone.

"I want to speak to Mr. Tip Martin," he said when he had the number he had dialed. He felt a surge of fire go through him as he said that, because Tip Martin was the biggest and cleverest racketeer in Hollywood. He owned a night-club, but behind it was an organized and lucrative business. Martin always bragged that everything he did was within the law.

"Everything except murder," the Human Rabbit told himself.

The Human Rabbit was only a fair acrobat. He had earned the hated name for his trick of leaping over rather high obstacles—leaping like a rabbit. As for a stunt man, though he worked the most steadily, there were plenty in Hollywood better than he. In spite of this he was distinguished. He was distinguished because he was the most hated man in the film capital, and he was almost proud of it. The fact was that he looked like a bantam. He was sleek, and greasy, he had bad teeth and a breath that stifled one, and you probably would not have let him eat in your kitchen with the colored maid. He was ugly. He was repulsive. And he knew this too. But what he had was a brain, a loud voice, and a smart shyster lawyer in his employ.

He never went into a person's past, yet he could intimidate the most chaste saint, or the shyest young virgin in the business. His methods were foul but he either worked them in such a way a person could not directly blame him, or they would not arrest him because they did not want his proof, false or otherwise, revealed.

Now he was waiting to speak to a man who was, in a way, in the same business as he. A man who hated him perhaps worse than anyone else in the business—Tip Martin.

"Martin speaking," came a cold hard voice.

The Human Rabbit said, "What have you done with Barton Boyce, and what's the meaning of this telegram?"

"What the hell are you talking about?"

"You damn well know what I'm talking about," said the Human Rabbit, "and this time, Martin, you've gone too far. A deal is a deal but I didn't ask for murder."

"Murder?" Martin echoed.

"That's what I said. Boyce is dead and you know it. I'm going to see you get what's coming to you. I may be afraid of breaking the law, but I have no fear of you, and I think I'm the only man who has guts enough to tell you that!"

Martin's voice softened. "I owe you something, Rabbit," he said.

Mart Brown was a little surprised. "Owe me something?"

"Yes," Martin went on, "a funeral and a headstone. I'll put in the order now." He hung up.

The Human Rabbit hung up the telephone. He fumbled for a cigarette. Maybe it would be better, he thought, if he left town for a while.

YOU HAD TO admit that Tony Key was good looking. Something like a combination of the best features of Ricardo Cortez and Clark Gable. He wore a blue suit, white shoes, a white turtleneck sweater, and had black hair that was like patent leather. His eyes were black too.

He had followed every false lead there was on the Boyce

disappearance case and he was tired out with it; and since it was a habit to concentrate while he amused his hands and eyes with less consequential things he sat back in the swivel chair in his private office now and sketched on a piece of white paper. He used a special instrument when he did this and called it a "candid pencil." He was not a bad artist, and sometimes he used his art on cases.

"Some day, Betty," he said to the girl who was his private secretary, his model, and his sweetheart, "I'm going to get real arty and do you in the nude."

"Not if I know it," she said.

"Modest?" His right eyebrow raised a little.

"No," said she, "particular."

He was handsome, but she was beautiful. Really beautiful. He spent half of his time keeping her away from casting directors. As a matter of fact she had been on contract as a stock girl when he hired her. She was platinum blond, had big blue eyes, white skin, and crimson lips. She had what Tony called the "best chassis" in Hollywood, and over this chassis now she wore a black, tight-fitting dress that accentuated the poignance of her shapely curves. She was standing, holding an apple on her head, while he sketched her.

"Look, Tony. Isn't this just a bit silly? I mean, fun's fun and all that—"

"Shh," he shhed, "I'm thinking."

"That's swell," said she, "all I need is a rose in my mouth and a fountain bubbling over me."

A bell buzzed. He looked up.

"Someone's in the outside office," she said, breaking the pose. She came over and glanced at the paper on which he had been drawing. There was no picture. Just the printed letters that had been traced and retraced: "What the hell. What the hell. Where is Barton Boyce?"

She said, "I stand there with an apple on my head while you— All right! All right, Tony!" She left the office and slammed the door after her. He picked up the apple and took a bite out of it.

In a moment she was back with a telegram in her hand. "Hey, that kid's here again. That brilliant young lad from Western Union who's been trying for two weeks to date me for lunch. He said for you to read this while he waits. He said you would want to see him."

"Did you tell him I was in San Francisco?"

"Yeah, and you know what he said? He said: 'Don't kid me, cutie,' Some kid all right. They call him Sonny."

Tony Key tore open the telegram. His green eyes flickered as he read it. "Send the kid in."

"If you hire him," said she, "I quit."

"Betty, send him in!" He was a trifle irritable.

Betty Gale departed and returned with Sonny Lloyd. Sonny stood at the door staring at (the great) Tony Key for the first time. His hat was in his hand and he was blushing.

"You wanted to see me?"

"Yes, sir. I thought you might want to check up on that message and I wanted to tell you not to do it. It would cost me my job."

"You mean it's a joke?" Tony demanded.

"No, sir. Only I took it to three other people. The same message, I mean. And I wrote that one—the fourth one—for you."

"Why did you do that?"

"Because I've suspected for a long time that you were a detective—the world's highest paid detective—and I wanted to see if you were. I knew if you were that you would like to know about this telegram, too."

"I told him you were just an agent," said Betty Gale.

Tony looked at her. "You probably sounded very convincing when you told him that. The way he believes you."

"I'm a smart kid," said Sonny. "I find out about a lot of people. I don't want to get Miss Gale in trouble."

"Ah, romance," said Tony. Then he grew serious. "I can use a kid like you occasionally, Sonny. I mean you can keep working for Western Union and when I need you, run a few errands. There'll be pay of course."

Sonny Lloyd swelled with pride. "Then you *are* a detective!"

"You don't know that," said Tony, "always remember, you don't know that."

"Oh, yes, sir!"

"Now I want you to tell me to whom you took these other telegrams and all you know about them."

Sonny told him.

IT WAS FIFTEEN minutes of eight, and Tony Key and Betty Gale sat on a little round stool that faced the fountain in the drugstore on the corner of Wilshire and LaBrea. They had been sitting there, off and on, for an hour and fifteen minutes.

"If I have another fudge sundae," said she, "I'll lose my girlish shape forever."

"God," he answered, "that would be terrible. You wouldn't have *anything* then."

"Thanks, Einstein."

He slipped off the stool. "Stick here. Make a date with the soda jerk if you think you have to do something. But stick. I'm going out and see what happens."

He walked out the front door, stopped and lit a cigarette. Half-way between the corner and a theater that was a few doors down, a large white circle had been painted on the sidewalk. A little sign in the center of it advised the public to keep out, and the people of Los Angeles, used to anything, did keep out, and paid little attention. Now and then there was a curious glance, but that was all. No one Tony had asked knew from where the circle had come. This morning when the stores opened it was there, that was all.

Tony Key glanced up and down the broad avenue. Wilshire Boulevard made the Fifth Avenue of New York look like a back alley so far as swank, and width and beauty went. From Los Angeles all the way to the sea it was flanked by huge modernistic stores, apartment houses, hotels. Now, ten minutes of eight, it was half crowded with people. People who seemed busy, yet in no particular hurry. The lights of the theater flickered merrily, and Tony noticed the picture on the bill was one he had seen.

In a moment he noticed a large blue sedan drive up. A man climbed out of the back and helped a girl to the curb. Tony saw that the man was the tall, curly haired George McGeorge. The girl was a small cinema youngster-star, Marian Cox. The car remained at the curb but McGeorge and the girl walked over to the circle and looked at it curiously. The writer glanced at his wrist watch and said something to Marian Cox.

They stood then, looking up and down the street, as though they expected to see Barton Boyce any minute. Pedestrians passed back and forth unaware of the promised drama for eight o'clock.

McGeorge and Marian Cox were still the only ones near the circle at three minutes of eight when Tony Key left the front of the drugstore and moved toward it. He saw that they were nervous and anxious. It was just then when it happened. Something black flashed before their eyes. There was a smacking sound, a loud crunching. Pedestrians turned. Women screamed. An object had fallen squarely into the center of the circle.

Tony Key reached it almost at once. Though the body was crushed and broken he recognized it as that of Mart Brown, the Human Rabbit!

RADIO POLICE CAME at once to hold back the crowd, but the wagon from the morgue took incredibly long and there was wild confusion. Marian Cox kept saying: "I'm so glad it isn't Barton. I'm so glad," and George McGeorge telling her: "I knew it wasn't. I told you I knew it wasn't. I have hunches." And the curious comments of the people: "Who was he?" "What happened?" "Suicide, eh?" "Oh, my God, it isn't my Jacob?" "No, it isn't your Jacob."

Tony Key listened to that while he stooped over the body and, without touching it, looked it over very carefully. Betty Gale had come out, wormed her way through, and was at his side. He thought she was worst with her constant reproof:

"You should have known something like this would happen. You should have known that when you saw a circle on the sidewalk. You should have gone up in the building."

"For the love of God, did *you* think of it?"

"No. I thought it was Barton Boyce. I thought it was a snatch and they were bringing him back."

"Since when," Tony asked, "do kidnapers deliver their victims in white circles, and since when do kidnapers snatch guys like Boyce who are practically penniless?"

"I dunno. But you—"

"None of us knew what was going to happen," Tony clipped. "This building has ten stories. Am I supposed to break into every room and search it for you?"

"No, but—"

"Look, Betty. The reporters are breaking through. Give out Mart Brown's name. Say suicide. Poor health."

"O.K., boss."

He sighed as she left him and went on examining the crushed corpse of the Human Rabbit. The shoes were upturned and he saw on the soles of them whitish marks that had been smeared with dirt. There were also stains of something Mart Brown had tried to wash off his hands. But that was all Tony could get. The body was somewhat of a mess.

He pushed out through the crowd and entered the building. It was filled with offices. There was a board with two hundred office numbers on it, but there were only a few names behind those numbers. The building was over three-quarters empty. Unrented!

"Well, anyway," said Betty's voice behind him, "the building makes a nice decoration for Wilshire Boulevard. Like a pic set—beautiful as hell, but nothing behind it."

He turned. "Talk to the reporters, Betty?"

She nodded. "And I've even found the elevator in this place for you. There's nobody to run it except a friend of mine who happened to come into the drugstore shortly after you left. I hope he'll do."

"Of course *I* couldn't run it," grumbled Tony.

But when he got to the lift and saw Sonny Lloyd standing, bright and shining, at the controls, he grinned. Tony said, "From the looks of the corpse I would say we want about the sixth floor, but there's an open window on the seventh."

"Seventh," said Sonny solemnly.

It was the seventh, and as Key had expected, it was unoccupied, and barren of furniture. For that matter there wasn't a single rented office on the whole floor. Key unlocked the door and stepped in. Betty followed him, and Sonny Lloyd waited.

Tony glanced around, his green eyes flickering. He lit a cigarette, and exhaled smoke through his nostrils. The floor was bloody. In the center of it lay a contraption that resembled an automatic fishing spool. It had a rope in it that ran to a pulley attached against the top of the open blood-stained window. On the end of the rope there was a hook.

"This is?" Betty asked.

"A way for the murderer to watch his murder," Tony told her softly. "Notice he has plenty of slack rope. He attaches the corpse to the hook, turns on the automatic fishing spool and beats it. By the time the spool has wound in all the slack the killer can be downstairs. On the sidewalk standing around the square maybe."

"You mean the circle."

"All right," he snapped, "don't get technical. I'm trying to explain this."

"Well," said she, "I already see it. The slack gives the killer time. When he is downstairs the rope pulls in to where it

Murder at Eight / 129

drags the corpse. The corpse is dragged up to the pulley on the window top. The hook jars against the pulley and naturally won't go through. This action causes the hook to be torn away from the body it was hooked in, and the body, being in the window now, falls. The killer, downstairs, sees the body thud on the sidewalk. It must be a lot of fun. But I suppose it's something that you just have to develop a taste for."

"Yeah," Tony replied, "like wrestling."

He had picked up the hook and was looking at it. He turned it over and stared at it strangely.

"What's the matter?"

"I'm either nuts or a bum detective," said he.

"You're both," she told him, "but explain."

"The hook," he went on, "has no blood on it. According to our theory, in order for this machine to haul the body up into the window the hook would have to be attached to something stronger than clothing. Under an armpit, or something. When the hook hit the pulley the jerk would tear away skin and there would naturally be blood. Follow?"

"Yes. And there's none?"

"Not a drop."

"Well," she offered, "it may have just happened that way."

"It may have," he said.

She asked, "Not to get away from the subject, but where is Barton Boyce? And what about those telegrams?"

He arched his right eyebrow. "Think about it," he said, "then you tell me."

"I probably will before we're through. I don't know what you'd do without me, Tony."

THE NIGHT-CLUB OWNED by Tip Martin was crowded when Tony Key entered—leaving Betty Gale with the hat-check girl—and made his way through the tables back to Martin's private office. He paused at the door, but he did not knock. He opened it and walked in.

He was immediately flanked by two huge, hard-looking gorillas who stood, immaculately garbed in tuxedoes, with their hands on something in their righthand jacket pockets. Tony looked at them coldly, then glanced across the mahogany desk at the heavy framed man who sat behind it.

"This is personal, Martin," said he.

Tip Martin's piggish eyes flickered dully. He too was dressed in tuxedo, but he looked somehow different from the other two. He had high cheekbones, and a heavy, squarish jaw. His lips were thick, and brown. He picked up a half smoked cigar, puffed on it, and regarded Key.

"Next to Human Rabbit Mart Brown," he said softly, "I hate you. And since Brown is dead—"

"News travels quickly," Tony snapped. "The papers haven't broken the story yet."

"Don't you suppose I have friends who use the telephone now and then?"

"I didn't know you had any friends," said Key. "I still want this to be personal. Do the boys here go, or do I?"

"What is that, a threat?"

"You've got murder over your head," Tony told him. "Figure it out."

Tip Martin dismissed the gunmen. Then Tony Key sat down and lighted another cigarette. He looked up through a cloud of smoke.

"We've played around in a feud for a long time, Martin," he said. "You've been pretty clever, keeping, as you put it, inside the law. I've locked up plenty of men I am certain worked for you. Nitwits who went to jail rather than to even whisper a word against you. Guys you had bluffed. But your rackets are mostly shake-down and petty graft that, so far as individuals are concerned, haven't raised too much fuss. You've worked smoothly—"

"What is this?" Martin growled. "You going to give me the Pulitzer Prize for outstanding criminal achievement?"

"No," said Tony quietly, "I'm just telling you that it's all over." He reached inside his blue coat, into the shoulder holster that rested against his white sweater, and palmed a blue-black automatic. "I'm taking you in for the murder of the Human Rabbit."

"You're bluffing!"

"No, I'm not."

"What evidence have you against me?" Tip Martin demanded savagely.

"None," said Key, smiling, and looking at his gun.

"Then—"

"The police have been known to invent evidence," he went on, "when a known criminal whom they can get nothing on commits murder, and they can't prove that either, there are ways of forcing the hand of justice. If you follow me?"

"But I didn't kill Brown!"

"You practically said you did when I came in."

Tip Martin got to his feet. His face was red, and ugly. "Listen, Key, if you think you can railroad me, you're crazy. One thing I don't play around with is murder. If you think you can take me to court and get a bunch of crooked cops to send me up, you've got another guess coming! Remember I've got one of the smartest mouthpieces in the country. Try any stunts and he'll have you and the whole Los Angeles police force out on your ears!"

Key had been bluffing and closely watching the results of it. He was satisfied.

"You didn't kill the Rabbit?"

"I'd say I didn't, of course," Martin breathed, "but, by God, this is true! I didn't."

Tony put his gun away and got to his feet. He came over to the desk and picked up one of Martin's cigars. He smelled it, and put it in his pocket.

Martin said, "Special brand. Made up for me. Hope you choke on it." He sat down, and began to breathe normally.

Key suddenly pointed his finger at Martin and raised his voice: "Listen, Martin, what I want to know is the connection between the death of the Human Rabbit and the disappearance of Boyce. I want to know that, and I want to know it damn quick!"

"Calm down," Martin replied. "I'll tell you just so I can wash my hands of this whole thing. I don't want any more to do with it."

"Well?"

"The Human Rabbit had doctored a reel of Marian and Boyce. Running around Malibu in the nude. That stuff. You know. They had bathing suits on originally, but he was a smart little guy and got pictures of real nudes. Trick developing. It must've been a long, tedious business and only the Human Rabbit would have the patience to do it. But I must say he did a damn near perfect job of it."

"It must've taken him months. He had a reel like this? Where is it now?" Tony Key asked.

"He's got it at home for all I know. But I've got one, too. He sold it to me to play in exhibitions."

"I want it," said Tony.

Martin said, "Don't be dumb. But, as I told you, I want to clean myself of this case, and I'll burn it for you. You can watch me burn it."

The phone sounded shrilly. Martin picked it up. "Yeah?" He looked at Key, then handed him the receiver.

Tony answered.

"Listen, boss," came the voice through the wire, "this is Curly Conley. Betty said you wouldn't need me for any strong-arm stuff right away tonight but told me to stay in the office and wait for a call. Been trying to get you all over town,"

"What's up?" Tony asked.

"Some punk called you up," said Conley. "He seemed excited as hell. Says he has to see you right away. He gave the address. Some dump hotel down on Main street."

"What's his name?"

"Barton Boyce," said Conley. "Yeah, that's it. Boyce. Said something about having been kidnaped."

Key hung up the phone and turned to Martin. "You can burn that film. And I mean burn it! There's a law against things like that, and you can't think of a damn thing that'd put you inside that law."

"I told you in confidence because you wanted to know about the Boyce-Human Rabbit tie-up."

"Sure. That's O.K. Let it ride like that."

Tip Martin got up. "Who was that on the wire?"

"Barton Boyce," said Tony.

"Boyce!"

"Yeah, been kidnaped. Well, be seeing you!"

He moved out of the office and into the night-club. The two body-guards of the gangster glanced at him and returned to the office. Tony found Betty Gale showing the hat-check girl how to pop gum.

She stepped in pace with him. "Something up?"

He said, "We'll see. You're going to the office and wait for me. Curly Conley and I are going to a hotel down on Main Street."

IT WAS EXACTLY twenty-five minutes of eleven when Curly Conley and Key hit Beverly Boulevard.

"Shall I turn on the emergency siren, boss?" asked the thickish man, Conley.

"We're all right," said Tony, weaving through two lanes of cars. "Be at the Second Avenue tunnel in a minute."

They were there in almost no time at all. The white tile wall of the tunnel swallowed them, but almost at once they were shooting out on the other side. They screamed across Grand Street, barely missing a taxi, and squealed to a stop at Broadway. The light changed and they darted on, passing Spring and coming into Main Street. Although only a block from the main district of Los Angeles the difference between this street and the others was almost like day and night. Main Street was the home of dime flops, burlesque, sideshows, quack medicine stores. It was dense with Mexicans, Filipinoes, and transient white trash.

They crawled past First Street, watching the numbers on the buildings. A half block later they pulled up in front of a hotel and stopped. Key climbed out of the car and his huge helper followed.

"I still think we ought to get the cops," said Conley.

"Didn't you say he said to come alone?" replied Tony. "You can't tell. Maybe he wants me to make terms with kidnapers for him. It seems to me that if he had wanted cops and had a chance to call—as he must have had to call me—he would have called them."

Conley did not answer, and in a moment Tony and he were climbing a dusty flight of steps. There was no one in the hole of a lobby. They arrived on the second floor and looked around. Tony Key brought out his gun, and Conley, watching, did this also.

"Nine, at the end of the hall, boss."

As lithely as a cat, Tony Key had begun moving down the threadbare rug. He did not like this silence. It oppressed him. He felt a moisture on his forehead that he knew to be sweat.

They reached room nine. The window at the hall's end was open and a breeze played in through it. Tony saw a rusty fire-escape, and not far from it, the sooty black wall of another rundown building. He stood at the door of the room and listened for sound. There was none. He could hear Curly Conley's labored breathing behind him.

Tony touched the knob of the door, turned it slowly; but the room was locked. Carefully, he slipped in a skeleton key, turned the lock, and quietly opened the door. Darkness gaped in, seeming endlessness ahead of them. Tony could not see through it. Gun gripped in his hand, he moved into the room. Curly Conley was right behind him.

Tony was three steps inside when he heard Conley's surprised gasp, then the heavy, wheezing groan, and the thud on the floor as Conley's body hit. Curly Conley had been slugged! Tony Key whirled, listened for sound to get aim, and when he heard a scraping of feet, opened fire.

Wham… wham….

A man moaned, thudded back against the wall. Then came his return fire.

The shot was wild, and Tony, realizing the man must be wounded, took a chance and drove forward toward him. He almost tripped over Conley. And then he became aware that there were two other men in the room. One slipped past him, and in the next moment cried out sharply: "Help!"

But the man who had sagged against the wall was pumping at his gun again, and pumping it at Tony.

Wham… wham….

Again the bullets missed and Tony Key thought the gunman must be a very poor marksman. He heard the glass of the window shatter, and then the lights went on and he saw the whole thing. The heavy, unshaven man against the wall, the gun gripped in his hand, the blood oozing from his side. He saw the glitter in the gunman's eyes, the blood that dripped from his mouth. He saw him taking aim again.

But Tony saw this while he moved. He was on the other, slugging with the butt of his own the hand that held the gun. The unshaven man's weapon dropped and crashed on the floor. But as this happened the other gunman brought his knee crashing up into Key's stomach.

Tony felt air rushing out of him, and then he saw a fist slough out and in the next moment it hit on the side of his face. He brought up the gun he had reversed in his hand, and just then it happened. Someone from behind, whom he had not seen because he had been too busy with the figure in front of him, came down with a terrible, splintering blow on the back of his head.

A cry choked in Tony Key's throat. He felt hot blood trickle to his neck, and a blackness, deeper than any blackness he had ever known in his life, formed a mirage over his eyes so that he could not see. He felt nothing, yet he knew that his legs had quit holding his body; he knew he was falling; and he knew he hit the floor hard, and that as he hit, his bleeding head jerked back with the impact. And then consciousness had left him....

But not for long. Not for longer than a minute, because he had gone out desperately aware that he must not go out.

The door of the room was open and he heard men in the hall, and a clanking on the fire-escape. He struggled to rise; he must follow.... But he could not rise. His muscles wouldn't permit him. He lay there aching because he could do nothing. He felt someone move at his side. He opened his eyes, and he saw someone: Curly Conley, shaking his shaggy, bloody head; grasping the bed post and trying to pull himself to his feet.

"God," someone on the bed was saying, "God, this is awful."

Tony Key looked at the bed and he saw a man tied up with heavy ropes. He wore soiled white flannel trousers and a torn shirt. His chest was bloody, and his head was bloody. His face had been beaten almost out of shape. But Key recognized him. It was Barton Boyce.

"Je-je-jeez, Tony," gasped Boyce, "It's yo-you!"

Tony wanted to laugh. He wanted to laugh because here was Boyce whom the police had hunted for three days and whom he had thought was murdered. Here was Boyce, and his abductors were gone. Here was the handsome silent-movie star, stuttering as ever, but no longer handsome. Tony tried to laugh, but his throat was too dry and blood choked from it. Every muscle, every nerve he had commanded, gave away. He lay there, unconscious, and still bleeding.

WHEN KEY OPENED his eyes he was still in the little hotel room, but he felt much better, and at first he could not understand this. It was not until he saw the interne putting the last of the bandages on his head that he realized he had been treated. After all, he had not been shot. Only slugged. But what a slug it had been!

Boyce had been washed and bandaged also, and he sat on a little chair in the corner of the room smoking a cigarette and trying to answer a dozen questions at once. Detectives had surrounded him, but it was Curly Conley who shouted his questions the loudest.

"Why in the hell didn't you call the cops?"

"Because I was hysterical," said Boyce. "I knew T-Tony's number by heart and—"

"How did you know Tony Key was a detective?"

"Be-because," Boyce explained, "a-a producer, Ha-Harry S-Sullivan, felt sorry because he co-co-couldn't give me a job and suggested I-I-I might get one working for Key. I promised I'd keep the fact that Key was a dick under my hat."

"That's right," said Tony from the bed, "he was around a couple of times. Only we never have had anything for him."

"I-I-I thought Key would understand and know the best thing to do," the tongue-tied blond went on. He had blue eyes that were warm, the kind Tony liked, and they pleaded now with Key. "I-I meant to do right," he half whispered. "I'm sorry for what happened."

The interne had finished and Key got up. He glanced around the room, stooped and picked up a cigar butt which he looked at. Near it, on the floor, was a note. He picked it up. It was addressed to Marian Cox and demanded five thousand dollars' ransom. One of the detectives had seen Key pick it up.

"The place is full of those things," the detective said, "Some of them only half written, some just started. The idea was that Boyce was supposed to write the note and he wouldn't. The kidnapers—he said there were three altogether, though there were only two here when you came in—tried to forge his writing but were never able to agree on a good enough piece to send."

Key's lips thinned. "They sort of beat you up pretty bad, didn't they, Bart?"

Boyce said, "Sort of. Bu-but, God! I-I couldn't ask Marian to pay ransom for *me!*"

"What happened? They left you for a moment and you got a chance to get to the phone? That was when you called me?"

"Not exactly," Boyce said, "two of them went out with the idea of making some contact with Marian tonight anyway. The one left to guard me hadn't slept much and he fell asleep in his ch-ch-chair." He nodded toward the phone beside the bed. "I-I managed to get to that. I could only talk for a minute."

Tony Key nodded, his green eyes flickering. He glanced around the room, then looked back at Boyce who was getting to his feet.

"Did you know Mart Brown?"

"The Human Rabbit? Yes."

"Did he have anything to do with your kidnaping?"

Boyce said, "I don't know that he did. I doubt it. I didn't see him. And they didn't mention his name. Wh-wh-why?"

"The Human Rabbit," said Tony, "is dead, and things are pretty screwed up." He sat down, jiggled the receiver of the phone, and gave the number of his office. Betty Gale came on the wire.

"We've got Boyce," Tony told her, "and we're coming back. Thought you might want to know."

"Tony, you all right?"

Tony Key grinned. "Sure."

"Well, I'm not. Have I been in a dither! Been trying to get you at every hotel on Main Street. You might have at least given me the address of the place!"

"I would have, if I hadn't been afraid you would follow me."

She snapped, "What am I? Your dog, or your secretary? Do I make a habit of following you?"

"Forget it," he said, "and tell me what you were calling about."

"About more telegrams," she answered. "Another load that Sonny Lloyd was given to deliver. Only this time *you* were put on the list by the sender. Sonny delivered ours and beat it. Says he has a lead on who sent it, or thinks he has. He's under the impression that because you want him to run errands for you that he's a detective."

"Forget little points and get to the big one. What did the telegrams say, and who got them besides us?"

"McGeorge and Marian Cox got them, too," she told him. "I'll read you the message. It's rather brief: 'My perfect performance will be repeated three times before eight o'clock tomorrow morning stop You will be one of the three to follow in the tracks of the Rabbit.' It's signed," she went on, "like this: Barton Boyce."

Tony Key stared over at Boyce, then at the phone. He felt suddenly sick.

"Haven't you any ideas?" Betty's voice was tense, "it's one in the morning now. Only seven hours left. I shudder to think that the murderer will probably be as punctual as he was at eight tonight."

"My only idea," said Tony, "and I'm *sure* of this, is that the killer is pretty close at hand. The killer is somebody we've done business with on this case already tonight. That doesn't make the solution easy, but it's a little better than searching the Hollywood hills for a maniac. Remember this hasn't been all touch and go. I've been doing a little thinking en route here and there and—and well, the main thing is, don't worry, Betty."

"That's easy to say. Not so easily done. When can I see you?"

"I'm going to take Boyce to Marian Cox," he told her. "Meet me at her house."

"O.K."

He hung up. He wondered if tonight he was going to be worth the money that made him the world's highest paid detective. Or whether at eight o'clock in the morning he would be a corpse.

"Ar-are we going?" asked Boyce.

"Sure," said Tony Key, "we're practically on our way."

KEY TOLD CURLY Conley to go back to the office, told him where to call in the event anything came up, then took Barton Boyce to the home of Marian Cox. He was a little touched to see the tiny young actress sob so with joy upon seeing Barton.

Betty Gale arrived shortly, and, of course, she had to tell Boyce about the telegrams right away.

"I-I didn't know that," the blond actor said. "Ma-Marian, why didn't you tell me?"

"I didn't want to worry you, darling," said she, "you've been through so much."

"But Betty didn't mind worrying you at all," Tony came in.

"Be-Betty was right," protested Boyce, "I should know. Death before eight o'clock. Oh-oh, my God! We-we have to do something about it!"

Tony Key crossed his knees, drew a pad of paper from his pocket along with his candid pencil. He began sketching, oblivious to the conversation that went on around him. He drew a round circle. In the center of it he put a pair of shoes, beside those, a hand. He then drew a hook, and after that a picture of a cigar. He put the candid pencil away and looked at what he had drawn. He studied the little figures very carefully. But he could come to no conclusion. Everything pointed in the wrong direction. Maybe, thought he, these clues were no good. Maybe he was on the wrong trail. The thought bothered him because he knew not where else he might turn. It was past two when he finally got to his feet.

"If anybody calls I'll be over at George McGeorge's house."

He told Marian and Boyce not to worry, said good-by and left. He climbed into his car, heard the door on the opposite side slam and glanced over to see Betty Gale sitting beside him.

"Going with me?"

"I'm staying with you until eight o'clock," she said.

He said, "I can think of nights when I would have loved to hear you say that."

She did not smile, and he shifted the gears of the car, and started moving down the hill. He coasted a while, then let the motor pick up. He thought it strange that Betty was so quiet. He glanced at her and saw that she was pale.

"What's the matter, skipper?"

She asked, "Love me, Tony?"

"I've always thought that I did," he said, and he felt her touch his hand. It was a nervous touch, and her fingers trembled.

He saw that the stars in the sky were turning pale, and that the moon was on the rim of the world. He felt the breeze of the night, and the moisture in it that would put dew on the ground. He saw palm trees, tall and stately, and unmoving; and the few lights that had been left flickering in Hollywood. He saw these things, and thought of them, and thought of Betty Gale. Something choked up in his throat. It was strange that he should feel like this. Perhaps it was the night, and the tenseness, and the strain they were under.

They crossed Hollywood Boulevard and he tried to shake off the feeling. They arrived on Sunset and turned right. In a moment they were pulling up in front of the house owned by George McGeorge.

"Did you follow a clue here?" she asked.

"No. A hunch."

She said, "Swell. One, two, three. Guess which. The world's highest paid detective. I think you're slipping."

"You're not supposed to think," said he, as they climbed out of the car and crossed the lawn. They rang, and the servant opened the door. He was tall, and lean and had a bony face. Tony Key brushed him back with his hand and Betty slipped inside the house. The butler seemed bewildered.

"Here!" he cried. "This is the residence of Mr. George McGeorge. This is—"

"He probably knows," a cold voice from the dining-room door said.

Tony Key looked up to see the tall, curly-haired author standing there in a blue smoking jacket. "Yeah," he said, "we already know. You got a telegram, and so did I. I thought I'd come over and compare shrouds with you. Do you like black, or is that too conventional?"

McGeorge ignored this. "If you think I need protection," he said stiffly, "you may as well—"

"It isn't that, handsome," Betty Gale quoted, "it's just that we didn't know where else to stop off at two in the morning."

"I have special police coming here at five this morning." McGeorge went on, following Key from one room to the other. "I think that measure is sufficiently precautionary."

Tony Key whirled and his eyes glinted with the hardness of green jade. "What special police?" he snapped.

"Why I—I—"

"Sure," Tony said. "I know. You were thinking of calling some. But you haven't yet. Maybe you won't need protection! You didn't seem surprised when I told you I had received a telegram along with yours. Maybe you knew about that too, though there isn't any way you could have learned, except—"

"Do you mean to insinuate—"

"Tony never insinuates," said Betty, "he guesses, and barks like hell hoping he'll scare you. But he's never muffed a case yet, even if he does like to pretend he's a question-and-answer detective now and then."

Tony said, "Thank you, Betty. You always say the brightest things. I don't know how you think of them." He walked over to McGeorge's study table, picked up a round tin can.

"It's all right," Betty replied, "no extra charge. Only if you're going to do something, I wish you'd lock this creative genius up. Until eight tomorrow morning anyway."

Key was looking at the can, and now his eyes came up and met those of George McGeorge. "The Boyce-Cox films. Where'd you get them?"

"Why, I—" McGeorge flushed red. "Marian gave those films to me to keep."

"You lie like hell!" Tony charged. "You went to the home of the Human Rabbit tonight and stole them!"

"Well? What of it? I wanted to get that reel before the police did. Brown tried to sell it to me for ten thousand. We were dickering. I wanted to avoid a scandal for Marian!"

"You broke into his house," said Key. "There's a law against that."

"I thought," snapped McGeorge, "that you'd be the last person who'd know anything about that. I didn't invite you in here, you know."

Tony handed the can of film to Betty. "Keep that." He turned and started going through the papers beside the author's typewriter. He picked up one sheet and looked at it. A peculiar light gleamed in his eyes.

"Write this?"

McGeorge looked at it. He could scarcely get his breath. "My God! No!"

Betty asked, "What is it, boss?"

"Rough draft of a scenario," said Tony. "Giving the details of a corpse falling into a white circle. It's dated yesterday. It looks as though McGeorge couldn't even resist the idea of selling the plot he had for murder."

George McGeorge was trying to catch his breath. "I tell you I didn't write that!"

Key picked up another sheet, folded it with the first, and put them in his pocket.

Betty Gale said, "What are you waiting for? Put handcuffs on him. What do you want him to do. Pull out a gun and start shooting just to prove the rest of it on him? Does he have to confess before you do anything?"

George McGeorge sank down in a chair, brought out a hand-kerchief and wiped sweat from his face. His features were drawn, his eyes were dull. "I'm innocent," he whispered. "I don't care what you do with me, I'm innocent."

Tony Key watched him for a moment, then glanced over at Betty. "I'd lock him up, sweetheart," he said, "but there's still something screwy on this case. The something that's been screwy since the beginning. I wish I knew what it was."

"I wish you did, too," she snapped, "another three minutes and I'll be screwy!"

The door bell began to buzz. It didn't cease. The buzz went on, endlessly. The butler who had been standing at the door turned and went to answer it. Betty Gale followed after him, Tony Key watched McGeorge. Key didn't know his own thoughts. He was confused.

Presently Betty Gale was back, and Sonny Lloyd was with her. Tony stared. The Western Union boy was so excited he was shaking. He tried to talk, but he got his tongue twisted up and for a half a minute stuttered. Then:

"I called your office and they told me where you were. So I came right over." He sucked in breath. "I've got news. Been working on this for hours. I found out who sent the last batch of telegrams. Positive of it."

"Who?" asked Tony.

Sonny Lloyd said, "A guy who owns a Hollywood night-club. His name is Tip Martin."

Betty Gale flounced down in a chair and threw up her hands. "All right," she sighed, "all right, get a straitjacket and put me in it. No, first get a drink. Something solid and hard that'll burn all the way down." She reached over and picked up a cigarette, put it between her pretty lips and lit it. "Here we are," she went on, "leading this literary lion of super pix by the hand in the direction of the noose, and—" Smoke swirled out through her nose. "What's the use?"

Tony Key was watching her, his green eyes slightly narrowed, his smooth face without a flicker of emotion. He was seeing pictures. A man falling into a circle on the sidewalk. Women screaming. Shoes, hands, a bloodless hook of iron; he heard the tuxedo-garbed Tip Martin, saying: "Listen, Key, if you think you can railroad me, you're crazy!" He picked up the echo of gun-fire from an old hotel room on Main Street. He remembered waking up with a bandaged head and seeing a tongue-tied blond actor sitting in a chair smoking a cigarette and trying to answer questions.

"Betty," he said quietly, "keep shush for a while. You rattle."

Sonny Lloyd seemed disappointed. "Ain't you going to do something, Mr. Key? This dope is correct, I had a hard time getting it."

"Sure," said Tony, "sure I'm going to do something. I'm going to my office and finish this case. Did anyone get wise to what you were doing?"

"Some of Martin's men might have," Sonny replied. "I had to ask a lot of questions."

"I see." Tony looked over his shoulder. "Coming, Betty?"

She did not move. "You're going to leave McGeorge here? Not going to—"

"I asked: Are you coming?"

"Sure," said she, and got up.

HE PARKED THE car on Hollywood Boulevard in front of the building in which he had his office. Betty walked across the sidewalk with him and into the elevator. The night man was fully seventy-five years old and since no one else wanted night service on the lift, it was Tony who had to pay his salary.

"Working tonight, I see," he said.

Tony Key said, "That's right."

They stopped at the fourth floor which was the top, and got off. The marble corridors were dark. Betty took Tony's arm, and they moved through the hall and around the corner in the direction of his office. They were twenty feet from the door when a pair of flashlights blinded them. In the next instant the lights were off, and there was darkness again. But only for an instant. Thunder and red hell and splintering wood, plaster and glass. It was a submachine gun.

Brrrt.... Brrrt!

"Dirty, rotten killer!" Key oathed. But the flashlights had given him warning. By the time they were off he had jabbed the full force of his right elbow across Betty Gale's jaw. She went out, and going out, went down, crashing on the marble floor. Tony himself flung his body forward; he landed on his arms and stomach. He was on the floor when those first two blasts came, and his gun was in his hand, had almost jumped from his shoulder holster to his hand. He raised it now.

Wham! Wham!

Brrrt!

The return fire of the machine gun bullets whined over his head. Vaguely, through this din, this seething hell, the world's highest paid detective heard Betty moan. Consciousness was returning. If she got up, if she raised so much as six inches....

Wham!

Brrrt!

The hall was ruthlessly demolished. Doors fell in, half cut in two, glass kept smashing, and falling, piece by piece. The halls echoed with the roar of the sound. Tony saw the lights in his front office go on. He saw the door open and a figure come out. He fired again—twice.

The light had faintly silhouetted the figure of the machine-gunner down the hall, and Tony Key had triggered at it the moment it came in view. He heard a groan. A thump, and then the crashing of the submachine gun to the marble floor. He leaped to his feet, rushed, half staggered forward. But there was a second gunman. His weapon bit out in short, staccato bursts that flamed red through the darkness.

Wham! Wham! Wham!

The three slugs shrieked past Tony. He was conscious of the wind they created; conscious at the same time of the figure who had come from his own office—Curly Conley. And now the lights in the hall flashed on. Key saw the dead machine-gunner, lying in his own blood, saw the last lone gunman standing over the dead man, a smoking forty-five gripped in his hand. Conley was right behind Tony.

Tony Key saw this picture; he saw it as his body careened forward. It was a flash, and then it was spoiled. He was on the gunman, he was on him, and bearing down. They were falling to the marble floor together. Falling over the corpse of the machine-gunner. Key lifted the butt of his weapon. He felt the gunman trying to struggle from under him. It was the same gunman-kidnaper he had seen in the room where they had found Boyce, the man that had gotten away on the fire-escape. Tony smashed down with his weapon. He saw the blood stream down the gunman's forehead, down into his eyes.

He saw this, then he felt Curly Conley behind him. Conley's strong arms lifting him off the would-be killer and setting Tony on his feet. Tony wiped sweat from his face and stared down at the unconscious man, looked over at the dead machine-gunner. Then he turned back, and saw Betty Gale with a black and blue lump on her jaw, dazedly getting to her feet. Tony was sweating, and shaking, and his heart was still beating fast, but he grinned.

"Boy, do you look sweet, honey!"

"Yeah," said she feelingly, "all I need is an apple on my head, then you can take my picture with your candid pencil."

The seventy-five-year-old elevator man came hobbling down the hall. "Lord! I heard the noise and turned on the lights. Think I should call the cops? Should I?"

Tony Key said, "I hired you on the condition that you were blind, dumb and deaf. I'm cop enough to take care of a pair like this. Get back to your car."

The old man nodded, gaped at the dead man, and hobbled away.

Curly Conley said: "Geez, boss, we didn't know they were out here."

Betty Gale looked as though she was going to answer brightly to this, but evidently she was feeling too badly. She pushed into the office. Tony looked at Curly Conley.

"Never mind that. I've got a job for you. This time you're going to earn your salary. I want you to go and get Tip Martin and bring him here. Tell him I have some questions to ask, and unless he wants to be wading knee-deep in boiling water he'd better haul himself over damn quickly!" Conley nodded, and started to speak, but Tony went on: "I'm going to shag somebody perhaps not so dangerous—Boyce."

AT FOUR A.M., the office of Anthony Key, whose door announced him as a motion picture representative, had never looked better. Betty Gale sat on Tony's desk, still dressing her jaw, and looking now and then in the mirror. The tongue-tied Boyce sat glumly in a corner smoking a cigarette. A corpse was on the floor. Beside the corpse, sat the gunman-kidnaper Tony had knocked out. He was done up in nice white rope, and in his mouth were seven of Betty's soiled handkerchiefs which did for a gag. His eyes were smoldering.

Tony Key sat behind the desk. He had been drawing pictures of everyone with his candid pencil. He did this, not consciously, but while he pieced the rest of the case together. Now he tore up the drawings and threw them in the waste basket. He looked at Betty for a moment, sitting on the desk.

"Look," he said, "the back of your lap is awfully pretty, honey;

but would you mind moving it to a more convenient spot?"

She moved at once, going to a leather chair and sitting down. She glanced at her watch. "It would appear that Curly ran into difficulty or something."

Tony said, "Conley may be dumb, but he's dogged. He'll bring Tip Martin in all right."

While he spoke he compared the scenario page he had taken from McGeorge with the other page he had lifted from the same basket. When he was finished he put both of the pages in his desk drawer.

"If Sonny were here," he said, "we could send him down to get some coffee."

"If that's a hint," Betty replied, "you'll have to get up and sing it. I'm not moving."

There was a sound in the outside office. Betty grew tense. Tony glanced toward the door, his hand on the butt of his gun. But he released the gun again the moment the door of the inside office opened. It was Conley.

Curly Conley's hair was a mat of bright crimson; his face was white, and drawn, and streaked with blood. His eyes were black, and half closed. His lips were swollen, and they, too, bled. He opened his mouth to speak, and blood came out of it, too. His clothes were in rags. He swayed there for a moment and then suddenly pitched forward.

Betty ran to him, Tony Key got up and looked down. But at that moment a cold, clipped voice said:

"Don't nobody move! Not so much as a hair. The first guy to get funny is going to get lead in the guts!"

Key looked up and his blood ran cold. Tip Martin stood there in a battered, dirty tuxedo; a scarred and bruised face; a face still unshaven yet glistening with sweat; a face with piggish eyes that glowed with the fire of hell and eternity. Cradled in his arm was a brand new submachine gun. His finger was on the trigger.

There was a terrible minute of silence. Boyce looked at the machine gun. Betty Gale stared, and did not move. The man who was tied up on the floor gazed blankly. Tony Key picked up a cigarette from his desk, put it in his mouth and lit it.

"Good morning, Tip," he said.

"Shut your lousy mouth!"

"I said good morning, Tip," Tony repeated.

"I sent the boys to do it," Tip Martin went on in that cold, hard voice that was strange, even to him, "and somehow they didn't, not even with a machine gun. But *I* can't miss."

"No. And you can't miss hanging for it after it's over."

"Don't try that stunt. It was in a picture called 'Blessed Event.' Only in life it won't work."

"Maybe not," said Tony Key, "but you'll still hang. Or do you intend to kill us all just to eliminate witnesses?"

Tip Martin did not answer.

"If that's the idea," Tony suggested, "why don't you go right ahead? Massacre the whole bunch of us. Boyce included, because he's really a nice guy, in spite of what happened. You know that, don't you? You know too, that you're so damned dumb you're letting yourself get all excited about something you might be able to get out of, as much as I regret it, unscathed. You knew I had the lead that you sent the telegrams and you thought I could build up a cinch case of murder against you. So you sent the boys to rub me out first. Now you come to do it yourself. You're worked up when you start toting those kind of guns personally. You think I'm going to send you to the gallows for Brown's murder."

"Well?"

"As a matter of fact I know who did kill the Human Rabbit and I know all about it."

"Well?"

"That being so," Tony went on, "what motive is there left for murdering me? I've already killed your pal over here, and I have the other tied up and in pretty bad shape. If you want to put your neck in the noose by killing me, just so you can deliver him back to freedom, you're sillier than I thought you were. Your friend," he nodded toward the tied-up gunman, "will go up for attempted murder. But so long as he doesn't squeal on you, I have no proof that he worked for you, and that you sent him. I know it, see? But I have no proof."

"You talk pretty, Key. Fancy as hell. But you ain't bulling me this time!"

"He never intended to," said Betty Gale.

"Shut up, fluff!"

"Listen," Tony snapped, "quit calling her fluff and put down that gun before you get in real trouble. You aren't going to use it and you know damn well you aren't. The longer you stand here the saner you're going to get, because I'm going to tell you exactly how everything concerning this case came about. Although no one told me, I'm going to tell you. The story comes from a neat collection of clues that have pointed in this direction from the beginning. But at first I couldn't believe them."

Tip Martin shifted the gun, blinked. "Well?"

Tony Key sat down and pinched out his cigarette. "The

Human Rabbit," he began, "was up to his usual tricks, shaking people down through every foul means he could devise. This time he got hold of some innocent moving picture reels of Boyce and Marian Cox. He fixed them up so that they looked pretty rotten. His first idea was to sell a reel to you; and then go to George McGeorge, tell him that he had the only reel—which was a print of the one he had sold you—and shake him down. After he had sold McGeorge one of the prints, he intended taking another to Marian Cox. Threaten her, and sell it to her, as the only reel. As a matter of fact, I don't know how he got the name rabbit, because I can think of a lot of others."

"Think of them tomorrow," said Betty impatiently.

"Anyway, Boyce, whom Hollywood has never quite succeeded in making sophisticated, and who at heart is still very noble and gallant, got wind of these pictures. He went to the Human Rabbit and what followed we can only imagine. Sufficient to say that Brown realized he would have to shut Boyce up and shut him up quickly. So he did. He slugged him. Slugged him so damned hard that Boyce was out for a couple of days.

"Meanwhile, the Rabbit, who had a brain like a fox, figured out how he could dispose of what he intended would be the body. It did not occur to him that Boyce would regain consciousness. He arranged the room in the building at Wilshire and LaBrea, arranged the hook and fishing gear so he could make the body fall out the window while he stood on the sidewalk and watched. This, he thought, would give him a perfect alibi for he intended to go up and clean up the room and get rid of the gear before anyone else found it. He sent the telegrams to Boyce's two closest friends, and to himself, so he could have excuse for being seen there while it happened.

Naturally, since he had to rush downstairs after fixing the corpse so it would fall, he had to be somewhere around, and he wanted witnesses for his alibi. Sending the telegrams to Boyce's friends, and wording the telegrams as he did, would also give the impression that Boyce had committed suicide."

"Th-th-that's right!" stuttered Boyce excitedly. "He's absolutely right!"

Tip Martin's eyes glittered. Betty Gale was sitting quietly, looking at her hands.

Tony Key picked up his candid pencil and began absently drawing. He went on: "But the Human Rabbit made just one mistake. He had left Boyce in the room on the seventh floor of the building, sure he would not regain consciousness. Boyce apparently did, however. He got his ropes off him, and was there, behind the door or somewhere, when Brown came in."

"Y-y-yeah!" said Boyce. "We fought like h-h-hell! I knew he meant to k-kill me! I-I got him to the window. We were still fighting. I-I guess I was so blind with rage that-that nothing mattered. I sh-shoved him out. I remember it was just before eight o'clock. About three minutes before."

"How did you know that?" Tip Martin asked.

"Clue," said Tony Key. "The hook the Rabbit intended to use was not bloody. It had not been used. Besides there was white paint stain on the bottom of his shoes, proving he had painted the white circle on the sidewalk. There were also paint stains that Brown couldn't wash off his hands. It was obviously his job, but I couldn't make sense out of it because Brown was dead and not Boyce."

"Easy, Sherlock," said Betty, "but what about the rest of it?"

"You should be able to figure that out," Key told her, "you're so brainy. Boyce was up in the air. If he had been sane and come to me, or the cops with his yarn, he might have been O.K. But he was a nice guy. Murder confused him. It's liable to confuse anybody. He was half crazy. If he had merely knocked the Rabbit out it might have been all right, but he had thrown him out the window. He could think of only one thing: Establishing an alibi for his disappearance that would clear him of the murder of Mart Brown."

"I catch." Betty said suddenly. "Let's see just how dumb I am; knowing something about Tip Martin, he went to him and begged him to fix an alibi. He knew Martin was shady and wouldn't turn him in. So Martin obliged by putting our tongue-tied ex-pic star in a hotel room with a couple of hoods. They fixed up fake ransom notes, beat him up a little more, tied him, and so forth. But he—Barton Boyce—called you, not the cops, to come down after him. They must have done the fake tying job after he used the phone. The hoods were supposed to fight you, so it would all be convincing, but they weren't supposed to bump you. And they didn't."

"Right," Tony told her, "as a matter of fact it was Boyce who smacked me on the back of the head when I got the drop on the hoods. You're right again about his hands being free of the rope. He smacked hard! Meanwhile, Tip Martin sent out the second batch of telegrams threatening dire things. This was to make us believe that the killer was still at large."

"How," asked Tip Martin, "did you tie me up to that room?"

"Because at one point you must have been in it. To see that Boyce got properly located. You dropped one of those cigars that you smoke. The special brand that you told me was made especially for you."

Betty asked, "What about McGeorge's scenario about the white circle dated yesterday?"

"I compared that page it was written on with another of McGeorge's pages. The bond of the paper is different. Brown wanted to throw guilt toward McGeorge and planted the fake scenario sheet there. Remember he was a rabbit and could get in anywhere."

Key looked at Tip Martin now. "Your motive, in case you are beginning to think that I suspect you of being full of charity and compassion for your fellow man, in hiding and making an alibi for Boyce was that you could forevermore hold the murder of Brown over his head. You figured Boyce would marry Marian Cox, who is making a nice salary, and you intended bleeding them for the rest of time. That's right, isn't it?"

Tip Martin's battered features flashed a grin in spite of himself. "Cripes, you don't think you're going to start being wrong now, do you?" He looked at the machine gun a little foolishly and put it down.

"That's right," Tony told him, "just leave it there. I'll blame it on your man Friday whom we have tied up there on the floor beside your man Thursday, the corpse. And as for bleeding Boyce and Marian Cox, remember I am listing the murder of Brown as self-defense. That's what it is. And that's between us. It would stand that way in court, but there is no need for that. It would only cost money, and involve a lot of nice people in some nasty scandal, and the Human Rabbit isn't worth that. In addition, it would make for rotten publicity and I'm paid a high salary and authorized to crack these kind of cases just to steer around such newspaper stories. That's all. The corpse goes to the morgue; the fellow tied up goes up the river for attempted murder. As for you, Tip, I hope you'll always remember not to press your finger against anything like a trigger."

"Ah, shut up," said Tip Martin. He looked around, and then he turned and went. The door of the outside office slammed.

"Wh-what about me?" asked Boyce.

"You go home. And if you ever tell Marian Cox about this I'll break your neck. She's just a kid, you know. You'd better be nice to her."

Betty Gale felt her swollen jaw. "Speak for yourself, John," she quoted.

Tony Key was very tired. He leaned back in his chair, picked up his pad and started drawing. He wished again, and aloud, for coffee. Betty went after it. In a while, a long while, everything and everyone had cleared out. The corpse was taken away, and the prisoner. Curly Conley was taken to the hospital where he would recover. Only the detective sat there; the world's highest paid detective, who sipped at his coffee and drew figures and symbols on white paper. He, and Betty Gale.

"Sonny Lloyd was out front," she said, "and wanted to know if everything was all right. I told him yes."

"He's a good kid," murmured Tony Key.

"Yeah, a good kid, and this has been something like a terrific case."

Tony looked up at her and smiled wearily. He saw the gray light of morning through the window.

"Yeah," said he, "terrific. And the only case I've ever had where the killer was dead from almost the beginning." He toyed with his candid pencil a moment, then he brightened: "Look, Betty! If you stand there by the window, and put that apple on your head, I'll bet I could do a honey of a picture of you!"

She said, "I'll bet you could, too," and didn't move from her chair.

Mystery at Malibu

Information by Sonny Lloyd
Solution by Tony Key
Murder by ——?

MISS GALE CAME in from her office and found Tony Key sprawled back in the swivel chair, with one foot on a drawer, and the other planted on the floor, making marks on a pad of paper which was in his lap. She paused, and on closer scrutiny saw that from this insane angle his focus was level with a fly which was standing on the glossy desk.

She said: "And you're supposed to be the world's highest paid detective!"

Without moving, and continuing to draw, the dark young man replied: "Don't come any closer. The platinum glint from your hair will scare him."

"Scare who?"

"The fly," he said, and added: "It is easy to see, Betty, that you don't appreciate my minor talents. To catch a likeness of him would be a victory in rapid sketching."

"Shoo," said she, and the symbol victory, pausing for one last lick of wings, flew away.

Tony Key looked up with green eyes that flickered with irritation. "Well?"

"We work late to keep up our files," she said, "and you draw pictures." She flipped a sealed envelope to his desk. "Sonny Lloyd bicycled it here all the way from Malibu… Shall I ask him in for sandwiches, or pay him now?"

"Nine in the evening," Tony Key remarked, "is scarcely the time for sandwiches. Pay him. And ask him, if you will, how he knew we were working late tonight? He knows more about what goes on in Hollywood than Hays, and I'm curious to learn how he does it."

"Fiddler and Winchell would like to know too," Betty said. "But I hear Western Union has renewed his option for another year. Postal was bidding for him, but W.U. closed at fifteen a week. Is that all?"

"For the present," said Tony, and he tore open the envelope. He took his white flanneled leg down from the drawer and moved closer to the desk. He read the letter carefully.

Dear Tony:

We are in a grave predicament indeed, and it is my contention that in a situation such as this you should be called, even though it is a case not exactly within the terms of your contract with the Associated Executive Producers Board, of which—as you know—I am a member. I have also considered that your presence here may arouse suspicion as to your amateur standing as a sleuth; and that some people may guess that you are not a picture agent, as, for the sake of keeping your identity secret, we have felt it imperative to represent you. Even so, I feel that you should come here at once.

The victim is not, was never, on contract to any of us, which legally lets you out, but because his murder may involve well known celebrities, I am of the opinion that the clause which states you will keep publicity of this kind squashed, is sufficient reason for you to take upon yourself the murder's solution.

I regret to state that the victim is Roy Standish, who was....

WHEN ROY CAME in, and he heard her laughter, and he saw, through the doors of the living room, the people who were present, his heart came up into his throat so that he thought for

"He just came in," said Ryan, "and he claims he doesn't know how it happened"

a moment he would suffocate. He was conscious of the butler taking his hat and coat, and asking his name, but he did not see the man, and for a moment it was impossible for him to speak. He wanted to turn and go, but even now it was too late, because more guests were driving up, and he could not get out of the house without being seen.

"Whom do I announce, sir?" asked the butler again.

"Announce?" the word was foreign to him, and he looked at the little man as though he thought he had lost his senses. Then he said: "You don't announce me. I'm the detective. The gun flunkey. I'm here to see that a Raffles doesn't steal the jewels. That one of our precious ladies does not fall into the hands of a kidnaper. I'm engaged for the entire week-end. I am being paid fifteen dollars a day. I—"

But Roy Standish stopped suddenly, for she was there at the living room door. Gloria Kent. He did not know how the words had come out of him and he flushed with embarrassment, though his face became cold again. He saw her beauty in hair that was gold on her shoulders, and eyes that were blue with laughter; but he saw her soul too, and he knew, uselessly, that he should hate her.

"This is a surprise," she said.

"It's awkward, isn't it?" he said. "I took the job without knowing that you, or any of your friends, were going to be here. The agency lied to me. I'll go now," he went on, "and tell them to send someone else."

"No, Roy."

His face was white, and bitter. "I wouldn't want to embarrass you," he said.

Her face blanched, and for a moment he saw in her not the star who had rocketed to fame in the past few months, but the girl he had known and loved at the beginning when he was a junior lieutenant on a battleship and she had come aboard with her company because she was playing a small role in a navy film. The music and laughter from the room swept him backward so that he heard the orchestra in San Diego. So that he saw her lips parted in the moonlight… and heard her laughter in the crazy house at Long Beach on the pike. He recalled the night he had put a diamond ring on her finger, and she had whispered: "I shall always love you, Roy, always." And after that her climb to fame, and his long cruises. Letters. And finally Hollywood talking about them. Pictures in the papers, and finally the producer saying: "You've always wanted to act? What have you been waiting for? A natural." The test film, then his resignation from the navy, a contract.

A contract which was never exercised, and whose options were never taken up. "Well, I'm better out of the navy anyway.

I'm a good flyer, and there's the air mail, and commercial ships. I'll get along." And the cold fear that had been in him during that month he felt Gloria slipping away, and at last Gloria saying: "I don't think we should see each other any more, Roy."

"You mean we're washed up?"

"Well…."

"If it's the job," he said, "I'll get on all right. It takes time, that's all. I—"

"It's not that."

"I see."

It had all happened so rapidly that he had scarcely been aware of a transition of time, and now he was taking anything he could get, and he was here facing her. The butler moved away.

"I want you to stay," she said, "I haven't seen you for three months."

He laughed, though not loudly. "Has it been all that time?"

She ignored this, and said: "I've been wanting to talk to you. I've been wanting to for so long! Frankly. Everything's been taken away from you hasn't it? I mean—"

"I'm all right," said Roy Standish.

"No. I know that you aren't." She moved closer, never taking her eyes from him, and her voice was a whisper. "Oh, forgive me, Roy, but I know you've been penniless, and it's about that that I have something to say. About your arrest. You see I was terribly hurt. But—it's all right now."

"Arrest?"

"Oh, I know, Roy. I know all about it."

"But you don't. I—"

It was inevitable that they could not be alone for long, and now a tall, dark young man moved out from the living room door. He was handsome, with wavy hair, and flashing eyes. He was Robert Lanthrop, the star. Roy Standish looked at him coldly, for he had known him too, before the columns had stopped linking his name with Gloria's, and had put Lanthrop's in his place.

"Well, old man," said Lanthrop, and extended his hand.

"You can save it," said Roy.

Lanthrop laughed nervously, and tried to pass it off. "If it's Gloria," he said, "she isn't going to marry me."

"We were teamed for a while in personal life for publicity," she said, looking up at Roy, "while they were building me."

Standish felt like a fool then, and shook the star's hand. "Come on in and join the bunch," Lanthrop told him. "We're waiting for supper. Ah, Jonas Jones. Look who we have with us, Mr. Jones."

Roy Standish shook the hand of the fattish producer and allowed himself to be taken into the living room. But he was trembling with new excitement, and he could scarcely wait to get alone again with Gloria so that he might talk to her. He greeted several people he had known, and sat down in the divan, Gloria beside him, and took the drinks as they were brought. He was flushed, warm with an exhilaration he had not known in months. He held Gloria's hand until her fingers were white with pressure.

"You're sitting beside the biggest box office find of the year," someone told him.

"That's right," remarked Jonas Jones, grinning broadly, "another six months of it and Merit Productions will be out of the red."

There was laughter, and outside waves crashing on a white beach, and the blood of the dying sun on the water. But Roy Standish had suddenly become uncomfortable for he was aware of Lanthrop, sitting across the room, staring at him....

... hired to keep his eyes on valuables, and guard the place while the rest of us slept. Conditions being what they are, our host wanted to take no chances, I guess.

We had just finished supper when the butler came in and announced that a man at the front door wished to see Mr. Standish. Standish went out on the porch, and the door was closed. We heard three shots. We arrived on the porch in time to see a car lurch away and speed toward Santa Monica. Standish was dead.

Because of the tremendous amount of unfavorable publicity that might be involved in this thing, I have taken the chance of not notifying the police. I have written this note because I didn't even want to talk about it on the phone. These local operators listen in for everything they can get when they know celebrities are in the house, and it is just as well that you take care of police details.

Please come at once!!

Jonas Jones.

"Betty, you got anything on a guy named Roy Standish?"

Betty Gale swept through the files, said: "Dead weight at Merit for ten weeks. No go."

"This note says he was never on contract."

"Do you call *that* a contract?" she asked.

Tony rose and slipped a black automatic into his coat pocket. "Get your hat, if you have one. And bring your pencil and note book. We're going to Malibu." He picked up the telephone and called Los Angeles Police Headquarters. "Mickey Ryan," he said, "homicide." When Ryan was on the phone: "Something else. Don't bring anybody along except the coroner. Malibu." He gave him the address.

NO ONE TOUCHED the corpse except to throw a table cloth over it, so it was still on the porch when they arrived. The coroner did the best he could under the poor light. When he got up he said: "He died, I would say, between eight and eight-thirty. All three of the bullets entered his stomach. I will send you a copy of my full report, Mr. Key."

Tony said: "That's all right."

Lieutenant Mickey Ryan, who was short, and had grizzly gray hair, snapped: "Who was the dumb bunny that didn't want to call the police? The guy's been dead an hour and a half!"

"An hour and fifteen minutes," said Robert Lanthrop. His face was very pale. "I happened to notice."

Tony Key looked at the crowd. "Into the house, everybody." On the way, he asked the butler: "Eight-fifteen, is that right?"

"It was about that, sir. Supper was just over."

In the living room, Tony Key smoked a cigarette nervously, and then when everyone was settled, moved up and down the carpet, talking as he walked. "I'm sure you people won't mind my questioning you. I'm only an agent who does amateur sleuthing, but Mr. Ryan, of the police, has asked me to help. Ah, Miss Kent. Miss Gloria Kent. Is it true that Mr. Standish had learned something of your past, or was holding letters you had written him—for money? Blackmail, that is?"

The pale young star sat with her hands folded, her eyes staring straight ahead. "Yes," she said, "I understand he was doing that."

"Did you ever pay him anything?"

"No."

"Did anyone?"

"I don't know."

"Who told you Mr. Standish was doing this?"

She looked up. "Robert Lanthrop. I was engaged at the time—engaged to Roy. He said I should know."

Tony Key's green eyes flickered. "You, Mr. Lanthrop. Where did you get your information about Mr. Standish? It wasn't a story you concocted to win Miss Kent, was it?"

"No. It was studio gossip that Standish was making the company pay through the nose."

"I see," said Tony, "but you *are* in love with Gloria Kent?"

"Yes."

"Did you ask her to marry you?"

Robert Lanthrop nodded. "But she said—recently—it couldn't be. That she was going to try and go back to Roy Standish no matter what he had done."

Tony Key put his cigarette in an ash tray, but kept his eyes on the actor. "Then she still loved Standish. But you felt that if it was not for him, she would love you?"

"Yes—ah—what are you getting at?"

Betty Gale looked up from her note book. "Motive, Mr. Lanthrop," she said. "Every murder is embroidered with motive…. Tony, isn't that about enough from him?"

"Yes," Tony replied, but Lanthrop leaped to his feet. "Do you mean to accuse *me?* Why, I was in this room when Standish was shot! We were all here. That can be proved!"

"Listen," barked Tony, "you heard the lady say we had enough from you." He turned. "Mr. Jones. Back to this blackmail. Did you pay off Standish?"

Jonas Jones' piggish eyes glittered brightly, and he folded his fat hands in his lap and nodded. "Twice."

"You know your company pretty well," Tony went on, "and most of these people are from your company. Can you supply any possible angles?"

"Ah—none. Except that we had a fleeting glimpse—though it was in the dark—of the man who drove off in the car after killing Standish. He wore a uniform."

"What kind?"

"I couldn't say. We tried to get the car's license and failed." Jonas was a big man, though he gave the impression that he was all flesh, no bone. His hair was gray, and thin; a bald spot shone faintly through the thinnest part of this hair. Rimless spectacles on a little gold chain hung from his coat, but he seldom wore them. The loose flesh on his cheeks looked pasty. He had a big name in Hollywood, and he would probably go down as one of its pioneers, though most of his success was in the past, and only recently had he made a come back.

The butler, who had an incredibly young and shrewd face for a servant, said: "Yes, sir. I also saw the uniform."

"Maybe a cop did it," Betty Gale offered.

"Listen," said Mickey Ryan of the police, "that ain't funny, and if we're looking for a uniform, there's one hanging around the foyer."

TONY KEY HAD begun to get ideas, and he sat down in a big chair and took a half empty cocktail glass which lay near him and drank down its contents. "Bring in the uniform, Mickey," he told the detective, and as the little man departed, said to Jonas Jones: "I once heard a rumor that you were in love with Miss Kent. Anything to it?"

Jonas Jones' eyes twinkled. "You never know about those things," he said.

Mickey Ryan returned to the room with a tall, good-looking marine captain. The officer was a blond, with a square cut jaw, and hard gray eyes; he was in full dress.

"He just came," said Mickey Ryan. "He saw the corpse but doesn't know anything about how it happened."

"That's right, sir," the marine said.

Betty Gale ran her hand around her platinum hair and studied the officer. Suddenly she said: "I get it now! You're William Seegal. Regularly attached to the marines, but running around with a star, and trying to crack the movies. Just like Roy Standish. You knew Standish in the service, and once you two had a fight on Vine Street in front of the Derby!"

Tony Key gazed at her in awe. "You're marvelous, Betty. How do you do it?"

"Well," she said, "much as I love glory, it was really that Western Union kid who squints from looking through too many keyholes, and makes gossip his specialty. When he picked up the letter here to take to you, he naturally saw the corpse on the porch. That's an angle our friend Jonas missed."

"I didn't miss it," Jonas came in, "I bought his silence for fifteen dollars."

"I always thought he took graft," said Betty, "but here's the story: he said he saw that Standish was dead. He remembered him because he had been linked with Gloria Kent, and also because he had seen him and Seegal fight once in front of the Brown Derby. Sonny told me all this when I tipped him for bringing the letter. He said the reason he thought of it was that coming out on the road to Malibu, which is not very crowded at night, he saw a green sedan streaking in the opposite direction. A marine officer was at the wheel. I didn't take much stock in the story, because I thought he wanted a bigger tip, but there it is."

Captain William Seegal's face was dead-white. "This is—is preposterous, I—"

"You did fight with Standish?" Tony Key asked.

"Yes. But I—I couldn't have shot him! I was driving in from San Diego and just now got here."

"*Why* did you fight with him?"

"He was trying to warn me away from Hollywood, and we had words about the service. We—"

"Did you go to Annapolis, Captain Seegal?"

"Yes. I knew Standish there."

"I see. That is all." Tony Key looked around for another cocktail, and seeing none, lit a cigarette. "Go to it, Mickey," he said to the city detective, "the case is yours." Mickey Ryan took the cue and began questioning everyone in sight. Tony sat quietly for several minutes, then got up, and unobtrusively slipped out and to the door. Betty Gale was on his heels. When they were on the porch, he turned.

"Do you get it, sweetheart?"

"Get what?" she asked.

"The set-up," he said. "The identity of the killer. It's the clearest thing I ever saw. Only we've got some work to do first. I want you to go down to Western Union and see Sonny Lloyd.

Ask some questions. Borrow a car, because I've got other places to go. And by the way—tip Sonny this time."

She said: "All right, if you say so."

TONY KEY WALKED into the wardrobe department at Merit Productions. The watchman wanted credentials, and Tony showed him the old badge he had left from the Federal Bureau of Investigation from which he had resigned. After that it was all honey and sugar. Tony went through the chits taken out for costumes (you had to sign for something when you took it) and found one signed by Joe Spioni. He put this in his pocket and left.

After that he drove over to Sunset Boulevard and down to the Tip Top Club, which was legally owned, but illegally run, by one Tip Martin. Martin had a pull somewhere and had scraped through a half a dozen raids on his gambling wheels upstairs without losing more than a couple thousand dollars in fines. But he had more than a gambling room. All by himself, he was Hollywood's constant crime wave, though it was said he never went in for kidnaping or murder, and Tony Key had never been able to get anything on him. The floor show was on when Tony came in and he had to break through it to get to Martin's office. He walked in without knocking.

Tip Martin's face was as ugly as his reputation, and he looked up scowling. He pulled a short cigar out of his mouth. "What is this, Key?"

Tony Key's green eyes were cold and hard. He lifted the automatic from his pocket and put it down, though out of Martin's reach, then he leaned across the desk.

"You lost a rod man last month, and imported another one from New York. A punk by the name of Joe Spioni."

Martin's face glistened with sweat. "Who told you Spioni worked for me?"

Tony Key said: "No one. I guessed, hoping you'd pop like that. You've never failed yet. What I want to know is, where is this Spioni?"

"So you want to know? You *really* want to know?" There was a frozen grin on Tip Martin's face, and he put the cigar back in his mouth.

"I want to know so badly," said Tony, "that if you don't snap pretty soon I might pin a murder on you. The D.A. could think of a lot of nice things to bring up about you, Tip. And I'd personally see that you didn't get bail."

For a moment the silence hung heavily, and Martin stared into Tony's eyes, then he said: *"Murder?* You know that ain't my line, Tony." He shifted. "I didn't bring Spioni here for that. If he's been taking jobs on the side—

"Give me the address," said Tony.

"Eighty twenty-three Flower Street."

Tony Key picked up the gun and held it level in his hand. "All right, now get up. How much longer does that floor show last?"

Martin, rising, said "It's just started, and it's forty minutes long."

"All right," Tony repeated, "now back over by that pipe. If you try anything I swear I'll let you have it. Arms behind you—around the pipe." He snapped handcuffs around Martin's wrists. They locked him to the pipe. "If the music out front sounds off key," he went on, "it'll be you yelling, but it isn't likely anybody will realize that until I get to Spioni's apartment." He threw the key to the handcuffs on the desk. "It's not that I actually think you'd telephone Spioni and tell him I was coming, Tip, it's just a matter of routine. You understand, don't you?"

"You dirty rat!" said Tip Martin, "I'll kill you for this!"

JOE SPIONI WAS much easier than Tip Martin. He was in bed asleep, and he didn't even have a gun. Tony Key hadn't thought it necessary to bother about a search warrant and using a pass key he had let himself into the room, then he turned on the lights. He kept the automatic in his hand and told Spioni to get up and get dressed.

Spioni had a greasy face, and curly black hair. He looked at Tony sullenly, but neither surprised nor frightened, and began to dress. Tony used his spare handcuffs on him, cuffing his wrists in the back. He noticed that Spioni was just past twenty, and said:

"Do you want to talk, baby?"

"Talk about what?"

"The shooting you did tonight. Do you want to tell who hired you?"

"I don't know nothing about no shooting," said Spioni indignantly. "I haven't even got a gun."

So Tony looked good for the gun and didn't find it. He said: "You had sense enough to ditch it, baby."

"I don't know nothing," Spioni repeated, "and you can't prove that I do."

"Well, we'll soon see," said Tony.

TONY KEY THOUGHT there might be trouble and

while driving Spioni out to Malibu, he stopped and picked up a traffic cop. He told the cop that Mickey Ryan would want to see him. They arrived to find the house dark except for a light that gleamed from the living room. On the porch, Tony heard the music from the radio, and above it the deep pounding of waves on the beach. The air was crisp and fresh, with salt in it. Betty Gale met them at the door.

"Tony," she said, "you look as good to me as Lanthrop's honey and syrup face does to a fan magazine."

"Thanks. You saw Sonny Lloyd?"

She nodded, and gave him a report. After that he had the traffic cop bring Joe Spioni into the living room. Spioni stopped at the edge of the carpet, and the cop stopped with him. The two of them stood there.

"Before we're through," Tony explained, "this guy'll be the life of the party. But he's always shy with people at first. Aren't you, Joe?"

"You can't prove nothing and you know it!" said Spioni.

Mickey Ryan looked at Tony, and got out his gun. The little detective's face was grim. Tony looked around the room, and the music seemed to be beating on his eardrums. He saw Gloria Kent looking white, and very frightened; the shine seemed to be gone from her gold-colored hair, and her lips looked too red. Her eyes were almost glassy. The good looking star, Robert Lanthrop, sat near her, his hands in his lap, his dark eyes shifting restlessly. Jonas Jones, with the dignity of an executive producer, sat back in a large leather chair looking perfectly at ease, though there was sweat on his fleshy face. Captain William Seegal of the marines was standing, one hand in his Sam Browne belt. The butler with the shrewd young face stood near Spioni, wringing his hands.

"Point the bloody finger of guilt," said Betty Gale, "they won't be able to stand this much longer." She snapped open her note book and poised her pencil.

Tony Key put a cigarette in his mouth. "It should be perfectly obvious," he said. He lit the cigarette. Someone turned the radio low, but the pound of waves still throbbed through the room. "Jonas Jones' life depended on getting Roy Standish out of the way!"

The producer lumbered to his feet. He looked at Tony, then looked around the room. "This is—is ridiculous!"

Mickey Ryan said: "Sit down, Jones," and after he had made Jonas Jones sit down, Tony went on:

"The circumstances which were to end in Standish's murder began three months ago when Jonas Jones, hopelessly in love with Gloria Kent, flattered himself that he would have a chance if Standish were out of the picture. That is, he thought if he could make her stop loving Standish, with his influence and all, he might be able to persuade her to marry him. It was as simple as all that, and at that time there was no murder in his heart. After Standish had left the navy he knew that if he didn't take up the option in his contract Standish would be in poor circumstances, and for a man in Mr. Jones' position it was simple to begin a rumor that he was paying Standish blackmail money for Miss Kent's letters; and to see this rumor, through Robert Lanthrop, got back to her."

Jonas was puffing. "You'll pay for this, Key!" he said.

"Of course when Gloria Kent heard this blackmail rumor," Tony went on, "she was too hurt to even discuss it with Standish and broke off with him. Though even if they had discussed it, it would have been very hard for Standish to prove that Jonas Jones' story was not true. Standish, of course, was crushed. But as time wore on, Miss Kent got over her hurt. This was because her love for him was—ah—well, the kind of love you sometimes hear about. She made up her mind that she would go back to Roy Standish. She told her plans to both Robert Lanthrop and Jonas Jones.

"I imagine when Jones heard he blew up. He probably told her what a dirty blackmailer Standish was, and because the story had spread, Standish would never be able to get on with any studio. He was poor, and had no future, except perhaps as a flyer on the air mail, if such a job ever came to him. Being an Annapolis graduate, and—shall we say a gentleman?—both Miss Kent and Jonas Jones knew that he would never marry her and live on her name and salary. She knew that with the way circumstances had turned out, she would have to give up her career if she was to become his wife. But between Jones' advances, the attention of Lanthrop which was forced on her, and the grind through which she had gone for so long, she was only too glad to do this. Ah, Miss Kent, isn't it true that you told Mr. Jones you were going to give up pictures?"

"Yes. I told him that I'd had enough. That I was going to marry Roy, and share Roy's luck."

Tony Key nodded. "Mr. Jones so badly wrecked Roy Standish's character that when Miss Kent told him she was leaving, he could not back down and give Standish a good job in pictures, and thus keep her also. His lies about Standish lashed back at him. He was desperate. He had once been successful, but for years he had lived in miserable poverty as a complete failure. Then someone backed him, and he was a success again.

"But this success was largely based on Gloria Kent's rise to box office prominence. She was making real money for him and he could see into the future where her tremendous success would pay off his debts and make him again the big man he had once been. But if he lost her, and he had just a little bad luck with his other stars, he might very well fail. He knew that if he failed this time he would never get another chance. Incredible though it seems, without Gloria Kent he was whipped and through!

"It must have seemed bitter to a man so ruthless and mercenary as Mr. Jones that for a thing so unimportant as love for Gloria Kent he had—in lying about Standish—wrecked what was now his only chance of keeping her. Obviously, he had to kill Roy Standish. Miss Kent would get over it in time, he thought, and having nothing to take her away, would remain in pictures."

JONAS JONES HALF rose, and sweat was moving down his fleshy face now so that it glistened. Mickey Ryan pushed him back into the chair.

"The rest is rather easy," said Tony. "Mr. Jones arranged to have the detective agency for which Standish worked, send him out here. Hearing there was a gunman in town by the name of Joe Spioni, he made a deal with him to do the shooting. To add a final touch, he too had known about Captain Seegal's fist fight with Standish in front of the Brown Derby, and he instructed Spioni to wear a marine uniform—at least the tunic—on the killing."

Spioni was livid, and glaring at Jonas Jones. The producer was trying to avoid his look, and said: "But me. You càn't prove anything on—"

"You were so hepped on the idea of a perfect murder," Tony Key cut in, "that you reasoned that after the shooting you might be nervous and unable to write the letter you intended to write to me after it happened. So you wrote this letter first—maybe a day before the party. Spioni was late, and by the time supper was over you were a case of nerves waiting for the fireworks. You thought Spioni should arrive any minute, and because you wanted everything to be just right, you went in and called Western Union to send out a boy to pick up a letter.

"Western Union marks down the time their boys leave and you called at eight, although Spioni didn't get there for the murder until *eight-fifteen!*"

Jonas Jones gulped. Great beads of sweat rolled down his fat cheeks. "I had another message—didn't call for that."

"Even so," Tony Key snapped, "Sonny Lloyd picked up your letter at eight-thirty. It was fairly long and written in ink. In the fifteen minutes that passed from the time of the murder until his pick up, *you wouldn't even have had time to write it!*"

Jonas Jones sank back in the chair and stared vacantly ahead of him. He was petrified. Joe Spioni screamed at him: "You dirty rat! You dirty, lousy, two-timing—" but the traffic cop shut him up.

Tony Key said: "Let's go home, Betty."

If Christmas Comes—

Joyeux Noel, Frohliche Weihnacht, Felices Navidades—but there is no Merry Christmas when Tony Key is on your trail....

THERE ARE A lot of things we like about Hollywood that the people outside don't know about, could not know about, because they are just the small every day things of living. They are things bigger than glamor and glory and money, that never make the publicity columns, and yet are the things that bring flesh and blood and breath to we who are idolized, symbolized, fictionized, and looked upon as immortal beings. In the days when I had to struggle to keep body and soul together, I used to think that money and fame would make a difference, but I know now that it doesn't; it makes it easier, but that is all. There is never anything different. So the little things, the elements around us that we see day in and day out are the things that count. They are the things that make us laugh and weep.

Things like the sunshine, and the careless freedom of Hollywood Boulevard, and the parade of girls in slacks, and the blondes who wait on corners and aren't afraid to be picked up if you wear a white sweater and have a Packard roadster. The little barbecue stands where you drive in, after a show, and have food brought to your car, and sit there and eat it and laugh far into the night. Like the beaches which are ordinary beaches but can be gone to either winter or summer. Like the mountains and resorts, and places to dance like the Grove, and places to eat like Musso-Franks where even Garbo will sit at the counter to eat her dinner. Things like open air markets that spray floodlights across heaven to advertise oranges ten cents a dozen; or the little movie house that has a surprize preview picture given to them an hour before the second show goes on.

Little things like those, intangibles all, count up, and mean something, and make Hollywood the best place to live and earn your bread in the whole world. The sentiment and the laughter, things too small to mention, things I cannot even remember—and then the very best of all these things. The day that makes the whole year worth living. Christmas Day in Hollywood.

If you ever went away, Tony, could you *ever* forget Christmas? There is no snow. There is only California grass and trees and flowers and the weather at its worst, but when you walk along Hollywood Boulevard you see Christmas different than you ever did before. In the first place it isn't Hollywood Boulevard then, it is Santa Claus Lane. All of the street signs are changed to that (remember?) and on each electric lamp for the entire length of the boulevard there is a color picture of a different star. You *are* a star when your picture is in the gallery along Santa Claus Lane because you're with the best this town ever turned out. You're with Marie Dressler and Jean Harlow and Rudolph Valentino and Lilyan Tashman—all of those great ones of today too: Mickey Mouse and Lionel Barrymore and Mae West and Clark Gable and Luise Rainer and all the others. You can see them all on Santa Claus Lane and you can see the ones who aren't posted and who are big. The producers and writers and directors and screen editors. You can see them in open roadsters. In the lobbies of hotels. In the doorways of apartments. Sitting in Henri's, or standing at the Brass Rail, or looking in at the Vine Street Derby for turkey like they never get at home. You can see success and failure and people drinking whiskey, which a director said was the "curse of a nation."

IT WAS LIKE that when I came on the boulevard at seven o'clock, which may be early in New York but isn't in Hollywood. You had called me, remember? I left the hotel as soon as I could get dressed. The drug store from where you had called was on the corner of Highland, but I thought I would walk. I would walk because it was Christmas and I wanted to see the shops dressed up, and the people who were also walking, but for a different reason than I. They were trying to walk off a hangover.

I remember now that I thought it was queer that you should call me because I thought of you only as an agent. A pretty good motion picture agent, I will admit, but no more than that. It was not until later when you started the investigation that I learned your agency was just a blind and that in reality you were a special studio detective. Rather, that your job was to put a heavy foot on the Hollywood crime wave in picture circles; and that made you the world's highest paid detective.

I came into the drug store, and you were standing there over the corpse. You were wearing flannels and white shoes, a white sweater and a black coat which is, I guess, the way you always dress, except that your patent leather hair wasn't so patent leather as usual, and I thought I saw trouble in your green eyes, or on your smooth-skinned face.

"Hello, Ben," you said. "Merry Christmas."

"Hello, Tony," I answered. "Merry Christmas to you."

"And Merry Christmas to a corpse," someone said, and I looked up and saw that it was Betty Gale who said that. Betty, your pretty platinum blonde secretary who has curves in the right places. "Hi, Ben," she went on, "how is Hollywood's most prolific scenario writer?"

"I am fine," I said, "who is dead?"

And then we all concentrated our attention on the corpse. It was that of a man, a little man whose hair was sandy and whose blue eyes—which were still open—stared glassily up and past us at some Christmas tinsel on the ceiling. I noticed he was lying there doubled up, and I said:

"How did he get it?"

"Poison," you told me. "He came here for an antidote."

"Yeah," said Betty Gale. "The poor dope was only about half conscious. Must have been whacky drunk. You know. When the store opened he wobbled in and asked the clerk how you could tell when you've been poisoned. He wanted to know how you could tell whether it was poison or appendicitis or indigestion."

"Then he dropped where you see him now," you said, "and he hasn't moved since. The druggist tried to work with him but couldn't. There'll be a wagon pretty soon to take him away."

I nodded, still trying to figure out why all of this should interest you; and why you had called me. I saw a bantam-weight guy with gray hair wandering around the store and you introduced him as Mickey Ryan of the Homicide Squad, but that wasn't until later.

"I suppose you wonder why we sent for you?" you said, and I noticed you were looking at your fingernails.

"Yeah," I said, "I *am* a little curious. Just a little though. It's a nice morning to be out."

"Don't you know the corpse?" you asked. I didn't like the sharp edge in your tone.

"No I don't, Tony."

Betty Gale shrugged. "Well, you can't always be right, Tony, my lover. You said Ben Thompson would know the stiff and he doesn't. So what? Do we pay his walking expenses back to the hotel?"

You looked at Betty and said to me: "Isn't it a shame? She's so pretty when she's quiet, too. You would never think she was crazy to look at her, would you?" You lit a cigarette. "Ben," you went on, "I did think you might know the guy, but that wasn't the real reason I asked to see you. Though Betty may claim that it was. The real reason is that I know you are sweet on a girl named Stella Mathews. That's right. You are sweet on her, aren't you?"

"Sure," I said, "plenty."

"Well," you replied, and I noticed a flicker in your green eyes, "it may surprise you to know this, but that guy on the floor was her husband."

I opened and closed my mouth. I was struck dumb with what you had told me. I honestly hadn't known a thing about it until you said it then. I stared down at the corpse and I still couldn't believe it. Stella was so young and naive; so sweet and—oh hell—you know all the words, and I know them, I've written them into enough movies to know them by rote.

YOU WENT ON: "Yeah, he was an assistant film cutter at Paramet, that's all. I got his name from his wallet. William Blake. Betty scooted back to my office and looked up the data on him. She's a good girl in ways like that." Then as though you had let something out, you added: "We have a file something like they have at Central Casting Bureau, only we list *every* studio job, not just the actors. We have the registered history of everybody here. Sometimes it comes in handy." You didn't say why it came in handy, and I thought at the time it was to help you place talent in the right places, which, as an agent, you were supposed to do.

"So Blake was her—her—"

"Her husband," you said. "I want you to tell us all you can about her."

"There isn't much to tell," I replied, "if you know what love is."

Betty said: "Tony Key never knows what love is at this time in the morning."

"I met Stella at the studio," I continued, as you arched one eyebrow at Betty. "She was just a little extra kid. I'm sure she was straight. If she had been married to Blake it must have been off with them, because I took her home once. She lived in a little twenty-five-dollar-a-month apartment on Kingsley Drive. One of those places that has a nice front, and inside, a fold-in-the-wall bed. Sometimes she didn't have enough to eat and I'd help her out. Gradually, as time went on, I fell in love with her. I don't know why or how. A writer who has been earning close to two thousand a week in Hollywood for five years has a pretty wide choice of women. But there was something about the kid that seemed straight and honest to me and...."

"And the bug bit you," said Betty.

"Precisely," I agreed.

You yawned and said: "Betty's right, this is one sweet time of the morning to be talking about love. But let's go over and see Stella." You turned to the bantam-weight Homicide detective. "See you in court, funny face," you said. "I'm going to walk around town a little on this case this morning, then I'm going to bed. Don't glut yourself on Christmas turkey."

"Don't worry about me," Mickey Ryan told you, "I do all right."

You and Betty and I left the drug store.

We drove over to Kingsley Drive. Stella was in red pajamas when she opened the door and I will say she looked neat. She had been in bed so that she hadn't a chance to wash her face, but it was the prettiest face for that time of morning I have ever seen. Her hair was gold on her shoulder and her eyes were as big as quarters, and bluer than the kind of sky they talk about in western pictures. She was a beautiful little tike. And I was very much in love with her.

"Ben," she said, looking at me in amazement. "What is this? It's not Xmas Eve anymore, and anyhow, I'm *not* having a party."

"Honey," I told her, "this is Tony Key. He has something to talk to you about. Tony is a big agent and if you treat him right you can't tell what he might do for you."

"No," Betty Gale came in, "you certainly can't. You can't *ever* tell about Tony."

There wasn't much more Stella could say and we all came into the apartment. It was a mess, all right, with the bed covers all wrinkled, and a man's pipe on the divan, a bottle of whiskey—

half empty—on the kitchen table. She had a little half-pint Christmas tree in the window and there were a couple of presents tied up in red paper and green ribbons lying underneath it.

Stella stood looking at us, and you told her right away: "William Blake is dead. Poison."

She went dead-white. Her hand went to her throat. "He—he—"

"Don't know," you said, "maybe he drank it accidentally, maybe it was suicide. He was pretty drunk when the end came. But from the way he was talking I think it was murder."

"Murder?" she echoed.

"That's right," chirped Betty. "Something they hang people for in this state."

You asked her: "You were married to him, Stella?"

"Yes," she answered frankly, "but—but we had separated. We didn't see each other anymore. It was something in the past that I thought I could bury and forget." I noticed there were tears in her eyes.

YOU MOVED ACROSS the room like a cat then, Tony, in your flannels, your coat, that sweater. I could tell that you had gotten an idea when she said that. You picked up the two presents from under the little tree. "For Bill," you read, then the other: "For Ben."

"For me?" I asked, and I gulped down a lump of pain that was in my throat. I didn't know that she was going to buy me anything, and it affected me quite a lot.

"Yeah, for you," you said, and handed me the package which turned out to be a green smoking jacket. I kissed Stella for it right there because she was already so nervous that she was sitting on the bed crying.

"Look," you went on, talking to her. "You've got to answer some questions."

That was when I interrupted and told you she had had enough for one morning. I asked you who you thought you were to take such authority. I guess I got tough with you. But you told me. You told me off then, and Betty added you were not only a detective, but the world's highest paid one. After that you went on with the questions.

"This present marked 'For Bill,' Stella. For Bill Blake, isn't it? William Blake?"

"I—ah—"

"It is," you said, "I know it is. Why did you tell me you never saw him anymore?"

"Well—on Christmas."

You were nasty: "I catch. You don't see each other all year, but on Christmas you exchange presents."

"Well—yes."

"Tripe," you said, "plain tripe." Then you turned and picked up the pipe from the divan.

"Pipe," said Betty Gale, "plain pipe." Then to Stella: "Honey, he's going to ask you to whom the plain pipe belongs. Have a good answer ready or he'll catch you up."

"It belongs to Roger West," Stella whispered, "his initials are on the bowl of it."

I guess we all looked up then. Roger West, like Clark Gable, was one of the really big stars. I thought she must have stolen it from the studio for its sentimental value, but she went on:

"I don't want to lie to you about anything, Mr. Key. Roger West was here last night. We had a few drinks together."

You put the pipe in your pocket, and said: "You get around, don't you, Stella?"

I was so shocked that I couldn't speak. She had never spoken of knowing West and though there was really no reason that she should have, I felt as though I had been cheated. I felt in my pockets for a cigarette. I knew Stella didn't smoke and finally bummed one from Betty. You were in the kitchen sniffing at the whiskey bottle. It sat among a lot of dirty dishes and wet cigarette butts that had turned brown, the color of the tobacco.

"Well," you said at last, "it's a cinch somebody poisoned Blake, and when we have the autopsy report we'll know what kind of poison. Meanwhile, Betty, my sweet, it looks as though we spend Christmas Day barking in blind alleys. Let's go visit Roger West." You looked at me. "Want to go, Ben? Or do you want to stay here with Stella?"

"I'll go with you," I said. "Stella's in no condition for company."

I just said that in front of her, but when I got outside I told you: "Listen, finding out what I have about Stella has made me pretty sick." This was the truest thing I ever said. "I want to walk it off or something. You don't mind, do you? The murder doesn't mean anything to me, but Stella does—or did. I'm all in a turmoil about her."

You patted my shoulder. "Okay, Ben, but if you want to go, don't think you'll be in the way."

"It isn't that," I said. "It's that I'm tired, and all confused. I want to walk—walk a lot. Then go home and take a cold shower and drink coffee. You know, when you called I rushed out without even changing my shirt—and well, I guess I'm pretty filthy. But I'd appreciate it though, on account of Stella, if you'd drop by and let me know how things turn out. Or Betty could phone me."

"Nah," you said, "we'll come over. Just have a good Christmas drink ready is all."

I WANDERED AROUND for a while, just as I told you I was going to, then I went back to my hotel. I was pretty blue. I wished that none of it had happened. I had been happy with Stella and now, knowing what I did, I didn't think I could ever be so much in love with her again. I smoked a lot of cigarettes and paced around. When it came two o'clock I tuned in Bing Crosby and heard him sing *Silent Night*, which he sings every Christmas. It's broadcast from coast to coast and across to England, of course, but that too somehow seems like Hollywood tradition.

I had changed my trousers and was wearing the green smoking robe Stella had given me, when you came in with Betty Gale. You looked pretty glum and flopped down in a chair, crossing your legs, and putting a cigarette in your mouth and lighting it.

"Roger West admits loving Stella," said Betty, "which would be swell copy for Winchell except that Tony is paid to keep down publicity like that as well as to solve murders."

She didn't make me feel any better, saying that, and I phoned down for Tom and Jerrys to be sent up.

You said moodily: "Outside of that, West was a fizzle. Couldn't get anything out of him."

"Yeah," said Betty, "I thought he was a He-Man, even though he's as handsome as seven hundred dollars. But he wears lavender pajamas, and doesn't smoke or chew, and eats oysters for breakfast."

We sat around, not saying much, then the drinks came up. They warmed us, the foam slopping over a little, and you perked up and said: "You know, Mickey Ryan, that little Homicide detective, has a lead, and I would not be surprised but what he was on the right trail this time. The only trouble is that Mickey can't figure a thing about the murder and doesn't know how to prove what he thinks. Well, we're all in the same boat. But Mickey has another film cutter—Wilt Davis—who everybody knows has hated Blake for years. Mickey and the rest of the cops have been questioning Davis. Just a little while ago they let him go."

"Since when," said Betty, "do you go around scavenging discarded police suspects?"

You wriggled your finger at her. "Tush, sweetheart. Cops have discarded killers before."

You got up, walked up and down the room. You stopped at my dresser and stood biting your thumb, though I don't think you saw the mess of junk on the dresser or anything else in the room. You were thinking. At last you turned.

"Well, I can't sit around and drink when there's murder doing. Up and going, Betty. We'll take a look in at this brother film cutter who they say had hatred in his heart that was like rattles on a rattlesnake. He worked right with Blake—Davis did, and—well, come on."

I was nervous and restless, and terribly blue. I thought anything would be better than staying in the room. I asked: "Can I go along?"

"Sure, Ben," you said.

So I put on my coat and shoes and followed along with you and Betty. I was beginning to admire the way you worked and I had taken a liking to Betty.

You remember what Wilt Davis' apartment looked like. It was pretty ritzy for an assistant film cutter, and the pretty brown-haired maid who answered the door didn't seem to fit the surroundings either.

"I'm beginning to see why these guys like their jobs," said Betty. "This is the next thing to elegant. And elegant is a special word with me."

When Davis came out you would have thought he was a producer instead of a film cutter. He was short, and heavy, and I remember how his eyes shone beneath the heavy black brows that were so prominent on his fat face. He was smoking a cigar; and his radio was playing a popular song: *I Get That Old Feeling*.

"Yes, I disliked Bill Blake," he said, "that isn't news."

"Any particular reason?" you asked.

"Several," said Davis, who was in an ugly mood, "but I see no reason for going into those particular reasons."

"Where were you last night?" you asked.

"Drunk," said Davis. "I was on a round of Christmas Eve parties and I got stinko. I don't remember what I did after midnight."

You went after him for more details, but he stuck to that story, and at last you said we might as well leave. When we were outside walking—the three of us—Betty remarked:

"I can see how the police failed to get anywhere."

YOU DIDN'T SAY anything, and we drove in your roadster back to Hollywood Boulevard. You parked in front of the drug store where Blake's corpse had been. We got out and went in. You stepped into the telephone booth for a moment. When you came out you looked at Betty, and told her:

"Cyanide."

"You poor fellow. What you want is a Bromo. Not cyanide. Imagine! So wacky he asks for cyanide!"

"Listen, my stupid platinum assistant," you growled, "cyanide is what they found in Blake's system. I just called the morgue."

"Oh," she said, "oh—that's different."

You lit another cigarette, and then we went out on the boulevard. We walked along without speaking and I was looking at the light posts and the pictures of stars on them and glancing about to see if I could spot any of them in the flesh. Then suddenly I noticed you had stopped. Betty and I hadn't noticed and were a few feet ahead. We stopped and came back. You were in front of a cafeteria.

"Let's go in for coffee."

"Coffee?" echoed Betty. "At this time of day? In *there?*"

"Lamb," you said, speaking to her, "because I give you eighty-five dollars a week and pin money on the side, is no reason you should spurn a perfectly respectable cafeteria."

So we went in, though she didn't feel like coffee and neither did I. This was an all night place, and at four in the afternoon—which it was now—it wasn't in any too good condition. A few sidewalk cowboy extras were having their turkey hash, but outside of that the place was empty. You drank two cups of coffee and kept looking around you, and I saw that same troubled look in your green eyes.

At last you said: "You two excuse me for a moment, please." You walked off.

"I knew two cups of that java would do that to him," Betty told me, and we laughed about it.

We laughed, but we were both nervous because we knew that

you were up to something and we didn't know what it was. It must have had something to do with the murder. It seemed to me that you had been acting queerly since leaving Davis' place. Twenty minutes passed before you came back and then if we looked into your face for some sign of expression, we were discouraged because you showed no concern. You sat down. You put a cigarette between your lips and lit it.

"Just take it easy, Ben," you said, "and sit here like nothing has happened, and pretty soon Mickey Ryan is going to come in and get you. I phoned him."

"What do you mean?" I said.

"I mean you brought Bill Blake here under the pretext that you were going to sober him up. You got coffee for him and put cyanide in it. Then, because you didn't want the doorman to see you leave you went into the men's room and out that window. When you come in this place you take a check from an automatic machine. The only time you are seen is when you go out and pay for the stuff they punch on your check. So you went out the window in the men's room figuring Blake would die right then and there and that that would be all there was to it."

"You're crazy," I snapped, "you're just crazy as hell, Tony! You can't prove that!"

"Listen," you said. "When you went out that window you jumped into the dirt down below. There's foot marks that'll fit your shoe."

"But a lot of men wear shoes my size!"

"Sure. But very few men have a check from this cafeteria up on their dresser, like you have. You must have dumped it there when you emptied your pockets to change your pants. If you had paid for your food you would not have had the check because they take them from you. And so you can't steal a check and come in and eat a big meal on a check that's punched for maybe a nickle. They have them marked by the day. A different color for every day. I spotted that on your dresser a little while ago. I took you along with me to Davis' because I wanted to throw the net around you slowly. I didn't want you to be suspicious. I didn't want you to have a chance to get out."

"What net?" I demanded.

"Murder net," you said, "can't you see that I have the set-up right now? You were jealous of Stella's husband and figured you had to get him out of the way. You and he and Stella were at her apartment drinking after Roger West left. West doesn't smoke and neither does Stella, but the kitchen is littered with whiskey-soaked cigarette butts and I put the rest together. The presents under the tree for both you and Blake. It all fits into a perfect picture."

I was gasping, trying to speak.

"I was first suspicious though," you went on, "when you made the break you did after leaving Stella's apartment this morning. I was first suspicious then and that's why Betty and I came back—*not* to drink your Tom and Jerrys. You said you were filthy, that your shirt was dirty because you hadn't had time to *change* it. You meant to say put on a clean one. But your tongue slipped. But the fact was clear: when I called you had just gotten in from the street and were still dressed. You were dressed, because an hour previous to that you had put the cyanide in Blake's coffee and had jumped out the window of this cafeteria."

Betty Gale was smiling. "And if you don't think that's a murder case, Ben, try getting out of it when they put the noose around your neck."

"It's a murder case," I breathed, "it's that all right. From such clues you trace my movements which covered hours. Oh, you've got something there. There's no getting around that." I straightened up and I guess my face was pretty pale, but I said: "Can't we go out and have a drink on it? One last good Christmas drink before that Homicide man gets here?"

SO I'M HERE in San Quentin now, writing this, Tony. Writing this and watching the hours tick past me. They say it'll never come, that they all hope the same thing, but I'm hoping for a reprieve. Hour after hour I keep waiting for it.

I have written this because it was on my mind and I had to write it, and because also it may be the last writing I will ever do. I was paid two thousand dollars a week for writing, and I guess the habit was too great to break. So maybe it was that. Maybe it was the writer in me that made me put this down on paper, although when I started out, I remember I had something to tell you. It was something I thought you should know, though it really makes no difference.

It was—oh yes—it was that a certain song I heard only once has been buzzing through my mind. The only words I know are those in the title, but they keep coming back. The title is *The Lady Is a Tramp,* and that's what I wanted to tell you. I didn't know Stella was really married to Bill Blake. She told me only that he was someone who had something on her and she hinted that she could never be happy until he had "gone away somewhere." It wasn't until I got up here that I saw the truth. I was obsessed with my love for her, and as Blake seemed to have some mysterious power over her that could make her do what he wanted, and because she cried about this, and because

I thought he stood in the way of my love, I killed him. I didn't tell her I was going to, so she is no way an accomplice, but I knew that that was what she wanted me to do.

It wasn't until I went around with you that I saw what it was. She was married to him and they were operating a little blackmail game of their own. He would do the dirty work and she would make up to big-money people like Roger West and myself and they would share the proceeds. But she was getting tired of splitting the money and tired of Blake, and seeing how nuts I was about her she worked on me to kill him. Subtly, of course. You couldn't pin anything on her in a million years. But she wanted Blake out of the way and that was her method. I was the sap. The fall guy. I did it for her. I killed him. But she was the instrument behind me.

I did that because I loved her, Tony, but she hasn't been around to see me, she hasn't even sent me a card; and I keep thinking of how sweet she was, then that song comes into my head. It keeps coming back all the time. That song: *The Lady Is a Tramp*....

Well, Tony, I guess that's all—only I keep thinking of Hollywood, and the little things that made life there, like the Barbecue stands and Musso-Franks and the markets that spray the heaven with lights to advertise oranges at ten cents a dozen— and of Christmas. It's so lonely here. Maybe I'll get pardoned. Maybe they won't hang me. But, Tony, if—if Christmas comes to Hollywood again and I'm not there... If I'm not there, take a walk down Santa Claus Lane for me, will you?

Me and Mickey Mouse

Camera! Lights! Action! Tony Key is on the set, solving the kidnapping of Baby Marie Dunn and the murder of her mother

1

HE RUBBED THE cold cream into his palm and smeared it on his face, leaning forward and looking into the mirror; looking at himself, and yet past himself, past the bare walls and into the future. But like the room, this stock actor's dressing room that anybody could use when he was working, he saw nothing in it. The future was as barren as the walls around him and he was a solitary figure walking into a mist that was nothing, and like a mist, fading.

This was the end. Today would be the end. The pretense, the sham, was all over. His fake laughter, his fake smile, his phoney slap on the back and "Hello, Joe," all of these he would lose. He would become a shadow like so many other Hollywood shadows, only he wasn't going to fake any more. If they asked him how he was doing he was going to say: "I'm washed up, that's how I am. I never did much. That is, I never did much in pictures although since I was a kid four years old I was eating my heart out to be an actor. And on the stage, once, they thought I was pretty good. They thought I did a fair Hamlet. They had begun to mention my name—Roger Dunn—along with Katharine Cornell and Alfred Lunt and Lynn Fontaine. Oh, doing that never got to be a regular thing, understand. It never went so far as to be a habit, and I was never accused of being nearly so good as they; but the beginning, the spark, the first notices, the insinuations, the vague hints, the admiration, they had all been there. That was what Hollywood saw. That was why I was imported but I was never used. The play they

brought me out to do was given to Barrymore finally, and then they got another script ready for me, a tremendous thing, they said, and it was that all right. They were spending a million on it. Only it was so tremendous that the last minute they decided because they were investing so much, and because except in New York, my name was so little known, that they'd better use Gable in the part."

He sat rubbing the make-up from his face, thinking that he would tell them that; he would tell anyone that wanted to know exactly that if they were patient enough to listen, if they really wanted to know why he was a has-been at twenty-eight, but of course no one would be interested. Yesterdays never interested Hollywood; it was tomorrows they worshipped, and tomorrow he would be through. It would all be over but the shooting. That was a good way to say it, wasn't it? All over but the shooting. Well, they might as well shoot him.

Anything can happen in
Hollywood—and usually it does

He smiled thinly, thinking of this; he smiled and dipped his face into a basin of water, and then began to wipe himself with a towel. When he was seated again he lit a cigarette and opened a drawer, glancing toward the door, and at the window, and then bringing out a bottle of bonded whiskey. He unscrewed the top and poured himself a drink. He took it down fast and wiped his mouth with the back of his hand. Then he got to his feet. He began to walk up and down. If he didn't do something he was going to go nuts. He had to *do* something, think something, he had to get all this bitterness he had kept his mouth shut so long about, out of him.

HE HAD TO do something so he decided to pretend that

someone *did* want to know why he was where he was, that is, up against the gray wall of defeat. He would pretend that someone wanted to know why his agent had just called up with that unmistakable note in his voice that was always there when somebody died or a contract ran out. Why his agent had said:

"I want to see you, Dunn, here in the office, just as soon as you're through work."

"What is it?" he had said. "Spit it out, Abe. Don't try to spare me. I guess I can take it. Don't act like I'm a woman who's a widow but doesn't know it yet."

Abe's voice had been cold: "It's better that we talk here in my office. The news is—well—ah—"

"Bad? Is it bad, Abe? Are they sick of seeing my face? Are they—"

He waited, but without hope.

"It isn't very good news. That's all I can say. Please don't press me, Dunn."

"No," Roger had said, "no—I won't press you. Not a bit of it, old man." Then he had hung up knowing that if Abe had anything that was even remotely hopeful to tell about his sad news that he would have come over to the studio to tell it.

So, thinking now, he decided he would pretend that some-one wanted to know *why* this circumstance had been brought about; why the brilliant Mr. Roger Dunn two years ago of Broadway had seen this coming, and yet was crushed by its arrival. He walked up and down in the room, reviewing the whole thing in the form of words, though they were unspo-ken words. He could do that, walk up and down, saying lines, without saying them out loud.

"After that Gable incident," he went on, "after missing out

on that it was one thing and another, postponements and stalls and my option ran out but was renewed, I don't know why, they kept thinking they were going to do *something* with me. Then because I had a lot of time on my hands, because I didn't know what to do, and because I was proud of my five year old daughter, proud of her beauty, and personality, and diction, I brought her to the studio.

"You've heard of her, of course. You know all that story about what happened. The kid made a million dollars in the first year. She has her picture published as often as the Dionnes did in the first year. They have Marie Dunn dolls and powders and baby soap. No nursery is complete without a Marie Dunn crib, and no baby warm without a Marie Dunn comforter wrapped about her precious hide. Mothers don't feed their children harsh laxatives; they feed them Marie Dunn candy syrup. Every time you turn around, in a bus, in a subway, on a train, on all the sign posts, on magazine covers, her curly hair and beaming smile leap out at you.

"That's swell, isn't it? That's wonderful. That's the height of parental bliss. That's the supreme happiness. Or is it?

"Wouldn't it look swell to see in big white lights: *Greta Garbo and Marie Dunn's father in Camille?* Not Roger Dunn. He's forgotten. Marie Dunn's father. They say he used to be an actor, that he had acting ambitions. That's what they say. They say when she was signed up he balked and raved and tore his hair and had all kinds of reasons for keeping a child out of that kind of life because it might spoil them, but mostly because it kept the child from being normal, and more than anything he wanted his little girl to be a normal little girl going to a regular school with other regular and ordinary little boys and girls. You might have heard about that? How his wife—Marie Dunn's mother—at once saw the magnificent possibilities to develop her daughter's talent, to bring out the finer qualities in her. Her mother saw this (or was it a lot of money she saw?) and put her foot down and insisted that Marie sign up. And that the studio changed Roger Dunn's name to Roger Watkins and put him on the stock actors' list at a hundred and fifty a week. Stock actors, you know. Waiters, one scene butlers, flash scene drunks singing to a lamp post. Color and atmosphere. What would the movies do without color and atmosphere? Without the stock actors?

"But whatever else happened it was certain that Roger Dunn, father of Marie Dunn, could never get very big because then Winchell or Fiddler would discover his identity and what would the public say? The public would say he was lousy. He had used his daughter to promote himself. On the stage, or on the screen, there would always be people saying that.

"So Roger Dunn went along being a stock actor, clinging to that much drama, trying to kid himself that he was, if not anything else, an actor of a sort. Sure, that's what I did. But all the time I've been waiting for the ax to fall. We've been kind, Mr. Dunn, but you're dead weight. Now your daughter is making plenty of money, and—this is just a suggestion, you understand, but don't you think it would be well if you—ah— retired to the sidelines? Going along, waiting for that.

"REMEMBER MICKEY MOUSE? Remember the tremendous possibilities he had? He and Barrymore were mentioned in the same breath. But then what happened? Disney played a lousy trick on Mickey. Disney brought forth a new offspring. And now it's Donald Duck you hear about. Donald Duck dolls. Donald Duck sail boats. Iron toys that walk and squawk named Donald Duck.

"So that's it, and now the knife has come, and I'm out, or I will be out as soon as I get over to see Abe. I won't even be able to go back to New York. Marie has me licked there too. But I shouldn't be blues singing, should I? I should be a proud and happy parent. I should be the happiest man in the world that my little daughter has so nobly endeared herself to the hearts of the public.

"Of course, this endearment cost me my wife. It cost me my wife because she at once became a financial wizard, a hawk hovering over a gold mine; our home turned into a kinder-garten in the mornings and a tea shop in the afternoons and a place for mad parties at night. It wasn't big enough, either. We had to move to Beverly Hills. Eighteen bedrooms and a swimming pool. And when Marie needed a week's rest she and mother flew to Reno to rest there, although it turned out to be six weeks and she came back and told me I didn't live there any more, but that I would be allowed to see Marie every Sunday between four and five o'clock. She didn't say I was to come in the back way when I came, but that was the idea. The pay-off came when 'Marie' made a monthly settlement on me. That monthly settlement is about all that's in the bank for her, saved for her, under her name, even though she doesn't know it. My ex-wife doesn't save anything, doesn't try to. Depressions are caused by people who save too much. Why should she worry? Marie will always be a star. She has her stardom all figured out in a ladder, year by year.

"So there you are. I'm out. I'm even going to be washed up as a stock actor in another hour. Marie Dunn and Donald Duck are the ones. Me and Mickey Mouse are out."

He stopped his silent speech and looked around him. For a moment it had been as though he was in another world. As though he were on the stage wrapped in a part and delivering an oratory that the critics would go home and write pretty adjectives about. But he was through now. The whole thing was out of him and he felt suddenly tired.

He dropped back down in front of the mirror looking at the circles under his eyes, and mechanically, as he did this, as he stared into his own pale face, he poured another drink. He poured it, and just as mechanically took it down. The cigarette he had put on the dressing table was burning into the wood and making an acrid odor.

2

HE COULDN'T SIT here forever. Life must go on. In one way or another the world must keep moving. Events had to keep happening; people had to be born, and people had to die. He had foreseen all this, hadn't he? He had been waiting for it, and now he wasn't going to lose his nerve and start spilling a lot of tears of self pity. Hell no. It meant only that the life time ambition and work of one Roger Dunn was finished. What was that? Think of all the Chinks in China whose lives had been finished right in the middle with a bomb. Think of all the starving extras whose dreams were more bitter than his, who had no talent but deluded themselves that they did, and were destined forever to failure. Think of all the people all over the country that wanted to be actors but would never get to Hollywood. At least *he* had had a taste. Critics had said he was good. The word genius had been associated with his name. He had *that* much to look back on. What was he kicking about?

He got up, thinking this, and grabbing the whiskey bottle. "Damn it," he said aloud, "damn it, I'm not getting Pollyannish, am I?"

It was tough, plenty tough, and he wasn't going to pretend that it wasn't. He went to the door of the dressing room and turned the knob but before going out he took another drink. He was beginning to feel the drinks now. Not only in his stomach, through his chest, but up in his head too. He opened the door and went out, conscious that his feet were heavier than they should have been.

He walked along the studio walk, the bottle still in his hand. He had done this so many times, walked on this walk, seeing the same things. The sound stages. The big fake sets. The people hurrying back and forth. But he walked, and without meaning to, without really making up his mind that he was going to do it, he came to sound stage sixty. It was closed up but he saw the guard sitting out in front of it, and he said:

"Is Marie working?"

"Yes, Mr. Dunn."

He felt self conscious talking to this man, the guard; he must have known. Probably everyone but he knew. He was a has-been. His chief claim to fame, at twenty-eight, was that he had a child.

"I—ah—I wonder if I could go in?"

"We have our orders, Mr. Dunn," said the guard.

"To hell with orders. I want to go in."

The guard got up. He looked hostile, but Roger met his eyes, and the guard said: "I'll go in and ask Mr. White if—"

"Yeah, you do that," said Roger. Then, when the guard had opened the door and gone inside, he climbed to the platform and slipped in through this same entrance. He saw the guard coming back. He hadn't even bothered to ask anybody. Roger slipped into the wings, drifted along the backdrops. The guard walked on past, went outside. He would probably decide Roger had given up the notion and gone on.

But Roger stood here for a moment, in the darkness, breathing and listening. All of the familiar sounds came to his ears. *"All right… we're ready for the take…* Mrs. Dunn, if you'll place Marie there on the box. Mr. Jones, is Marie's sweater right? Fine, fine. Lights now. Right wing arc. Now left. Now full…

Grips! Where is the grips? Ah, there you are… You at the camera. Have you got her in focus? Can you see her? How does she look?… She does, does she? Marie—Marie will you please smile now? That's it! That's fine. Do you mind moving back out of the scene, Mrs. Dunn?… Thank you. I think we're ready… Hey—that reflector. Get that damn reflector out of the way, what do you think we have lights for?… Ah, pardon me, Marie. Music, is the music ready? You strike a note when she says 'And the knight was filled with sweet cakes and music.' All right. Places everybody! Roll them, Howard! *A-ction.*"

He stood listening, hearing Marie say in a full, rich voice: "And the knight was filled with sweet cakes and music." Then hearing the orchestra, and Marie's voice as she sang, as her tiny feet moved in rhythmic tapping. He had thought he was alone and because he was absorbed in what he heard and what he was thinking he was not conscious of the girl who moved from out of the shadows toward him. When he saw her she was right beside him.

"Kathrine!" he whispered. The orchestra was loud, the mikes wouldn't pick up a whisper.

"Roger," she said, and she touched his hand so that he felt a flush in his cheeks. In a moment he was kissing her though he didn't know why he did this. She didn't mean that much to him. She was a stock actress, a nobody like himself, although a swell kid. She had beauty and talent and bad breaks. It was she who had stuck by him when his wife divorced him. It was she who had worked with him and kept him cheered. They had met at night too, to go to shows, to wander hand-in-hand up Hollywood Boulevard. To go to Tomayne Tommy's for baked beans, to sit home in the apartment he had taken and get drunk on gin. She was slim, and had rich red hair. But her skin, her beauty, was like a flame that licked in radiance from the smoky blue of her gown. She was wearing a gown in this picture.

"Roger," she was saying now, "what's the matter, you look sick."

"I am sick, Kathrine," he said.

She took both of his hands now, her eyes pleading with his. "What we've got to do is get away from here. We must get away from Hollywood. This life is killing you. The things you have to see and go through."

"But acting is my only life," he said hopelessly.

"There *can* be more than that," and her tone was impassioned. "Oh, darling, there can, and there must be more. Don't you see?"

HE WAS GOING to answer when he suddenly grew rigid with sound that hammered into his ears. The music had stopped. Marie's singing had stopped. The director was bawling. "Who in the hell is back there? Who in the hell is talking?"

Roger whispered: "You stay here," and leaving Kathrine he emerged. He stood in the giant flood lights with everyone looking at him. His ex-wife. His daughter. The director and his assistant and the script girl. The cameramen, and the grips, and the electricians. Then little Marie's voice broke, and she said:

"Daddy...."

He didn't care then; he went to her and put his arms around her. She was saying: "Did you come to watch me work, daddy?"

"That's right, sweet," he said.

He said that and just then Sara broke in. Sara, his ex-wife with her bleached hair, and her grimly-rouged face. "This is quite, *quite* uncalled for, Roger. This cheap display of theater dramatics in the middle of one of Marie's scenes. I do think, Roger, that you could have used more judgment. To upset the girl at a time like this, *really*...."

Roger whirled meaning to tell her to shut up, but he didn't. He just looked at her, stared into her shallow face, and then he walked on past her. Everyone was talking at once now. Obviously Mr. Dunn was dead drunk. Marie's make-up was ruined, didn't the fool know it took time to put on makeup? Well, that was a good way to burn up a half an hour of the studio's time, all right. Will someone show Mr. Dunn the way out. All of this he heard as though it was all blended into one giant voice, and then through it Marie calling: "Daddy, daddy, don't let them send you out again...."

But he did let them, he didn't have much choice. Four of the grips got a hold of him as though he was a confirmed alcoholic and was around endangering people's lives. The studio would never forgive him for this. He was thrown outside. He moved off down the studio walk.

He was alone again now, he was suddenly alone, and the bottle was still in his hand. He went around behind a building and took some of the whiskey down. He kept remembering Marie's voice when she said "Daddy..." He sat there drinking, remembering this, and then he got up.

"I'll see her if I want. They can't stop me from doing that?"

He said this, and aloud, but he was not sure. He was only sure that he was going to try and see her and talk to her. He was going to try and ask her a few questions, questions that circumstances had prevented him from asking before because he had thought they wouldn't be right. If her answers were as he thought, was sure now that they would be, he was going to court. Sara wasn't going to have her any longer. Sara wasn't going to ruin her.

He went around to her big dressing room where he knew he would find her "relaxing" for the renewal of the scene. He arrived at the door that was lettered: *Marie Dunn* and stood there for a moment, then he turned the knob and went in.

Even from the first moment he felt something queer in the emptiness of the room. Even before he knew there was anything wrong. Then he was walking, moving across the carpet. Sara was lying behind a big chair. Her body looked soft and made a half crescent as though she had cuddled up to go to sleep. But there was a gash in her head as big as a man's fist and blood had flowed from it in one big heavy mass that covered her face and matted her peroxided hair. A heavy cold cream jar was lying just beyond her head. The blow had been struck with this and had cracked the jar though not breaking it. Sara must have died instantly.

Roger Dunn stood over her corpse for a moment, feeling no emotion, neither grief nor joy nor even surprise. Then he looked up and around him in the empty room. He saw the note in front of Marie's mirror. It was lying against it. He crossed quickly and picked it up, but his hands trembled. It wasn't for him to open. He remembered that now. This was murder and he must leave everything alone.

Yet he knew that this piece of paper he held in his hand was a ransom note. He knew that Marie had been kidnapped.

3

CLARK GABLE IS without doubt one of the top actors in filmland; he turns in performance after performance of successes; little girls go to bed and dream about him; little boys, and some big ones too, wished they were more like him, looked more like him and had his personality. If this sounds like a fan magazine, skip it.

This is not a build-up for Mr. Clark Gable but for one Mr. Tony Key. It comes this way: when Mr. Key declared flatly that he couldn't act, didn't want any studio acting school or anything else to try and teach him, absolutely would not appear before a camera for love, glory or money, Mr. Gable came up and smiled that smile of his and shook Tony Key's hand and said he was frankly glad of this decision. It would make it a lot easier for them to both get along in Hollywood. Of course he said this as a joke and a lot of people, hearing about it, laughed. But maybe there was something to it.

So you see, after all, this build-up was for Mr. Tony Key. And no buildup of Tony Key would be complete without mentioning Betty Gale. Yeah, that's the way they were.

All right, *fade in:* Tony's office is on the fourth floor of a building on Hollywood Boulevard. It is a sumptuous office known to the general public as the office of a moving picture agent because studio executives deem it wisest to not let it be known that Mr. Key is employed by a pool of producers to work on, and squash the publicity of, all studio crimes from murder on down. The salary he gets for this makes him the world's highest paid detective.

He was pacing back and forth now garbed in a neatly tailored black suit and wearing beneath the coat a turtleneck white sweater. He always wore white shoes. Betty Gale came in from the outer office looking excited.

"Tony, guess what?"

He said: "You guess, honey. I'm in no mood for games."

"Okay," said she, "you asked for it. Here comes an ax right between your eyes: Miss Marie Dunn, age seven, star of—"

"Skip it," he snapped, "what happened to her?"

"Kidnapped. Her mother murdered. It all happened ten minutes ago; I just took the call. The producer was so excited he couldn't even wait for you to come on the wire." Tony was reaching for his gun, putting it in a hip holster, Betty went on: "You won't need the pea shooter. This is no mystery. Roger Dunn took it from his wife and the kid as long as he could then he went to town. They nabbed him right on the scene after he bumped his ex-wife. All they want us to do is to rush over there with our own picked Los Angeles detectives and keep the publicity out of the papers. They've got two of Marie's pictures hawking around the country and they don't want them squashed by publicity."

"I should think that a kidnapping," Tony started to say, sitting down and taking a telephone in his hands.

"I expected that from you, my brilliant Adonis," Betty said. "But tie murder with that. Sordid, isn't it? It would kill the kid's pix deader than a mackerel."

Tony Key, on the telephone, arched his left eyebrow, said: "You've got something there, sweetheart. Just what I'm not sure." Into the phone he said: "Detective… Homicide office? This is Key. I want Lieutenant Mickey Ryan. Right away…

What? Oh, I want to play a game of backgammon with him, yeah. You tell him that, will you? If you want any information you can get it from him afterward." He hung up, looked at the phone and added: "Maybe you can."

Platinum Betty was at the door. "You know, what puzzles me, Tony," she said, "is how, if they've already nabbed Roger Dunn and he did the dirty work, they can say Marie is still kidnapped. Sounds screwy."

THERE WAS A crowd in Marie Dunn's dressing room, but no cops, no one official. Max White, a director, stood shouting himself red-faced; an extra actor who had been a doctor's assistant once was bending over the corpse although he had no business doing it; and James Turner, a huge red-haired carpenter who must have had a cousin who was a cop, from the way he acted, was grilling Roger Dunn. Tony Key stood on the outskirts for a moment watching this horrible mess and feeling a hatred for the whole morbid crowd surging up through him.

"Come on, punk," James Turner was saying, "what'd you do with the kid? Don't give us some of that baloney about you don't know or I'm going to let you have one."

"I tell you, I—" Roger Dunn began.

"Shut up and tell us the truth," Turner roared.

Tony Key moved forward brushing people aside, said in a quiet voice: "That'll be enough of that, Mr. Turner. And will the rest of you please clear out? I've had a little experience as an amateur detective and although I'm only a movie agent, I'm taking charge until detectives arrive." He glanced down at the director who was examining Sara Dunn's body. "If you don't mind, fella, the coroner will probably save you all the trouble of getting your hands bloody. Besides, I understand there is a law about people monkeying around corpses."

"Go on," said Betty, "you heard Tony. Clear out, everybody."

The mob, that is what mob was in the room, needed only a leader, and now it had found one. Mumbling, one after the other headed for the door. The bald-headed director, Max White, still stood around, however, likewise the extra who had been examining the corpse, and also the red-haired James Turner who stood over against the wall quietly watching. Thomas Thurmas, the studio's executive producer, came in now, and behind him Kathrine Lewis who went at once to Roger Dunn and stayed with him.

Thurmas who was big and had bushy black hair, said: "Well, isn't this some mess, Tony?"

Betty Gale flipped out: "Don't bother him, he's reading the ransom note."

James Turner grunted: "Why read it when Roger Dunn wrote it and he's standing right here?"

Tony Key's white face showed no emotion, but his eyebrow flicked upward. "Shut up," he said. Then he went on reading the note. It was printed in ink and from the smudges on it looked as though it had been quickly penned. It read:

Let's have no foolishness about this. No newspaper headlines; no waiting. I mean business. I have neither the patience nor the cunning of a gang kidnapper. This is my first crime so I'm nervous and I really mean business. Unless forty thousand dollars in small bills is delivered to the outskirts of the studio Indian village, at the horse water trough, within an hour after this note is discovered, Marie Dunn will be killed. Any tricks and she will be murdered anyway. Despatch one person and one person only to contact me with the money and she will be delivered safely.

Tony Key looked up, his green eyes flickering. "Mr. Thurmas," he said, "you're the big man here. You always have an immense payroll for the extra talent who get paid every night. You must have forty thousand here—and in small bills too."

"You mean we're going to pay it?" Thurmas cried.

"Exactly," Tony clipped.

"But you're employed to see that—"

"Ah now, Mr. Thurmas," Betty Gale cut in, "nothing out of school. That's a secret, or isn't it? Anyway, if you did hire him you must have thought him capable. So don't start asking questions now."

"Why, young lady, I'll—" Thurmas looked ready to pop.

"Tut, tut," said Tony Key, "get the forty thousand and let's have no more talk."

"Marie Dunn isn't worth that to us!" Thurmas snapped.

Roger Dunn leapt across the room, his face livid. "Why you fat miserable punk! I'll— Not worth it! She's—"

Tony grasped Roger Dunn by the arm in a Ju Jitsu hold he had learned during his days as a Federal agent. He whirled him about, twisting his wrist, and sent him to the floor howling with pain.

"Another crack like that, kid, and I put handcuffs on you. I'm giving you a break as it is." He turned. "Get the money now, Thurmas, or I walk out on the whole case. I'm getting sick of this interference."

"I'll get it," Thurmas mumbled, "I'll get it," and he went out swearing under his breath.

TONY KEY LIT a cigarette, his green eyes burning. "Get out your book, Betty, we're going to town on this tribe." She jerked out a note book, flipped it back, poised her pencil. Tony looked at the large red-haired Turner. "You're a carpenter here, aren't you?"

"That's what they pay me for," the man answered. His face was broad, his eyes a slate gray.

Tony mused: "James Turner, studio carpenter," then he snapped out: "Just what gave you the notion that you had a right to grill anybody? You were grilling Mr. Dunn when I came in."

"I—"

"Never mind," Tony clipped, "just one more question for you, smart guy. *When* did you put on that pair of overalls you are now wearing?"

"I—ah—I'm on the afternoon shift," Turner said.

"The overalls were clean when you came to work then. Fine. Just a question. You look pretty crummy."

"Why I—I—"

"Oh, no blood, no paint, no real filth, just crummy," Tony went on. "That's all. Your absence will be appreciated."

Betty looked up with a wooden smile on her pretty face. "Goodby, Mr. Turner," she invited.

James Turner looked around, then he stomped out.

Tony looked up at Max White, the bald headed director. "What were you doing about the time Mrs. Dunn was dying and Marie was kidnapped?"

"I don't think, under the circumstances," the director said, "that is necessary to answer. I can prove where I was and what I was doing. Roger Dunn here—"

"Never mind Roger Dunn, I'll come to him."

"Yeah," said Betty Gale, not looking up from her book, "just concentrate on yourself, Mr. White. Who pulled out your tie, and tore your shirt?"

"I—I get in a frenzy when I direct and—"

"I think that'll do for you too, White," Tony Key said. "We understand about the frenzy. Maybe. Anyway that'll be all for now. I think the door is on your immediate left. Do you mind going out through it?"

As he walked out, Betty called after him: "We eliminate them fast."

She had just said this when Homicide Detective Mickey Ryan walked in. The coroner and a uniformed cop were on his heels. Mickey Ryan said: "Hello, Tony, what have we here?" but the coroner went straight to the body and bent over it. The extra who had been looking at the body and whom Tony had not questioned yet was still in the room, bending over the coroner now, watching him avidly.

Tony Key explained the setup to Mickey Ryan, and showed him the ransom note. It was then that the coroner put down his instrument and got up, his face white with rage.

"Who has been fooling with the body? And where is the instrument with which this woman was struck and killed? I would say personally it was a sledge hammer from the looks of her head. But—"

He gazed around accusingly.

The extra who had been watching the coroner suddenly began to move backward. His jaw worked back and forth but no words came out of his mouth. Then suddenly he jerked until he was rigid. A large, bloody cold cream jar dropped out from under his sweater and landed on the floor with a thud.

4

HE WAS A little man, the extra. Little but all muscle, like a miniature wrestler; he had a bony face, and brown eyes that were like spots of an amber drink spilled on an ashen white that was his skin. No one said anything now, they just looked at him, and the extra was both funny and pathetic. He stood, not daring to look down, trembling, sweating, as though he was waiting for a firing squad to open up on him. Then all at once he began to talk. The speech was at first a broken jargon but it gradually smoothed out so that parts of it was comprehensible.

"My name is Johnny Jones... Just happened to be working in Marie Dunn pix... Heard about this and—and came over. Once was in a hospital unit in the navy. Thought I could tell something about the corpse... I don't know what dropped out of my sweater but whatever it was I didn't put it there. I didn't know anything about it." He was silent for a moment then as no one spoke went on, slightly hysterical this time. "I *didn't* do it, I tell you! Why do you all stare at me like that? I'm Johnny Jones, just an extra, and I never hurt anybody. I—"

"Nuts!" Mickey Ryan ejaculated suddenly. The detective was a bantamweight with a red Irish face and gray hair. "Nuts, I say. You talk that like you rehearsed it, Johnny Jones. You're under arrest." He moved forward.

"Wait a minute," Tony Key came in. He arched his right eyebrow, glanced at Roger Dunn, and Kathrine Lewis, who stood by his side, then back at Johnny Jones. "Let him go, Mickey. Let him scram."

"What do you mean?" Mickey Ryan bellowed, whirling about. "It's against all police ethics. It's—"

"Let him go," Tony repeated evenly, quietly. "I've got a reason."

Mickey Ryan bit his lower lip, snarled at Johnny Jones. "You heard him. Go on! Get out!"

When the smallish extra had gone, Mickey Ryan said: "Well, Tony, you may be the highest paid detective in the game, but at this point I wouldn't say you were the smartest. The guy has the murder instrument hidden under his sweater and—"

Tony Key smiled thinly. "There would be no point picking it up, if he was the killer. Not unless it had his prints on it. And if Johnny Jones' prints are on it, it will prove that he is the killer, and that he *did* pick it up. But the way I shape things I don't think you'll find his prints on that jar. And even so, even if it turns out I'm wrong and he *is* guilty, we still don't know where Marie Dunn has been hidden, and locking up the killer at this point might be just like signing her death warrant."

Mickey Ryan thought about that for a moment, grunted: "I catch."

The coroner picked up the cold cream jar, looked it over, then wrapped it up to take it back to Headquarters for microscopic examination. "No doubt," he said, "this is the thing that did it. She was konked by somebody that had the punch of a bull. Or can you gentlemen see that?" He nodded all around, and left the room.

Mickey Ryan looked after him with his back to the others. Both Tony Key and Betty Gale turned and concentrated on Roger Dunn. The actor fumbled with a cigarette, put it between his lips, started to light it, then instead, dropped it and jerked:

"Oh, for heaven's sake, if this is an investigation, if you call it that, why don't you *do* something? My daughter is—is—why don't you find her? Sara is dead. Getting her killer isn't going to help poor little Marie!"

Tony said: "Take it easy, fella. I want your story. Everything you did this afternoon leading up to the murder. I've been saving you last because frankly you are the chief suspect and—well, I have an open mind. I hope you can clear yourself."

Roger Dunn looked around, picked up the cigarette he had dropped and lit it this time. In broken sentences, in a voice that was choked with emotion, he recited all that had happened, how his agent had called him, how he had been drinking and went to Marie's set, how he had come in here to find Sara dead and Marie gone.

Betty said right away: "You didn't get so drunk that you're forgetting anything?"

"No," Roger Dunn said. "No, I wasn't drunk at all. I was sick with headache. I was feeling down, so the whiskey did nothing for me."

Tony's green eyes had been concentrated on the floor, now they rose. "And you, Miss Lewis," he said, addressing the red-haired girl who wore the long blue gown, "Miss Kathrine Lewis. Did I understand from Roger's story that you two have—ah…."

She flushed. "We—we have found companionship in one another if that's what you mean. Oh, I'm sure Roger is innocent. Can't you leave him alone?"

Tony answered: "Sure," and took her hand, patting it. There was something about her wistfulness, the desperate sincerity of her love that he could not help admire. "Sure, and if things turn out right—I mean, if you're both clear, I hope you find a lot of happiness together." He kept holding her hand, squeezing it.

Betty said: "Don't take him seriously, honey, if he can lock Roger Dunn up he'll be around wanting to pay your rent."

Kathrine tossed her head and withdrew her hand. She glanced at Betty. "You should know more about that than me."

Tony Key turned, a flush in his face. "We're leaving the dressing room, Betty. You can stay and play kitty kitty with Kathrine if you want; what I meant was that I'm leaving." He looked over at Mickey Ryan. "See you later, bantam. Hold tight and don't make any arrests."

TONY MOVED OUT into the studio street, glad for the fresh air that bathed his lungs. It was dark now, and lights were gleaming from everywhere. A soft mist, not a rain, but heavier than a fog, had begun to drift from the sky. Betty came up beside him.

"What now?"

"A little incidental business," said Tony, "an idea I had. Then I've got to collar Thomas Thurmas and get that ransom money from him so I can keep that rendezvous."

"You aren't going to actually go out there to the Indian village lot with all that dough, Tony?"

"Sure."

"Alone?"

"Sure."

"But—"

"Listen, sweetheart," he said, "I don't intend to pay it out. I intend to clean the whole thing up. But I had to pop off in front of Thurmas like I did, just as though I was willing to pay, because the kidnapper—who is also a killer—was right in the room with us then." He paused. "I had to let the snatcher know everything was going along like he wanted it. See?"

Her mouth dropped.

"How did you know he was in the room?"

"You wouldn't understand," Tony told her, flicking his left eyebrow, "I arrived at the conclusion by using my eyes and observing an assortment of various little things referred to in a usual crime case as clues."

They walked along quietly for a moment, their faces dampened by the moisture in the air. At last Betty spoke. "According to character—if I have any after associating with you for the past two years—I should crack back with something smart. Like: which came first, the chicken or the egg—ah, I mean the clue or the crime. But I'm not going to."

"Thank you, Betty," he said, "thank you very much."

"I'm serious," said she, "honest to Pete, I'm serious, Tony. Now and then I get that way. I will say that you can observe more, find out more in a few minutes on the scene of a crime than—"

"Than you can. That's what you mean, isn't it? You want an explanation. You want to know who the killer is. Well, I'm not sure yet. All I've got is a lead and some ideas. All I know is how to proceed with the rest of the case." He was nervous, under tension as he always was in the middle of an investigation, and yet he was glad to have beside him the girl who had long ago become more than a secretary. There was something comforting about Betty, something warm in spite of her cold platinum hair.

They went into another dressing room now, one near both

sound stage sixty where Marie Dunn had been working, and near the dressing room from which she had apparently been kidnapped. Tony looked around, went out. Betty was still with him.

"There's Johnny Jones," she was saying, "that muscular little extra; there's Tom Thurmas, the producer, but you surely don't suspect him…. Ah, there's Max White, the director with the bald dome, and of course Roger Dunn himself, and that gal of his, Kathrine." She followed him into another room, a small wardrobe office which was now empty. "Tony, tell me, will you, whom do you—"

But she stopped there. He was leaning over a desk, picking up a blotter. He held it to the light, his green eyes flickering, and murmured "Ah!" Then he looked around, on the floor, at last stooping. He picked up a cigarette butt. It was tinged with both a pinkish color, and a dark blue both of which were smudged on it. He dropped this into his pocket and concentrated again on the blotter. It, too, was smudged with large blotches of ink.

"The ransom note was written in here. The noose is getting tighter around the killer's neck."

He said this, putting the blotter in his pocket also, and lighting a cigarette.

5

BETTY GALE STOOD there gaping, and then she said: "Sherlock Holmes was dim witted compared to you. And don't say Doctor Watson was clever compared to *me* or I quit right now and go back playing stock for Paramet. But what I want to know is how you could go along looking in various rooms and compartments and just walk in on a couple of nifty clues? You get a lot of dough for being smart like that, but this is beginning to sound like a dream."

"Look, my cherub," said Tony, "it was easy. I like to hear you say I'm smart but I'm just an ordinary guy, really, who's had a lot of swell breaks. It wasn't much to figure out the ransom note was written near here. From the way it looked, all smudged up, and in ink, I could tell it was done in a hurry. Someone in the studio wrote it, had to do it quickly before they were walked in on. Obviously they would have to write it in a place near Marie's dressing room. So here you are. And whoever wrote it wasn't so dumb either. Blotters seldom mean much and if you were in a rush they wouldn't mean anything. And that cigarette on the floor was a popular brand. Nobody could trace that. But I *did* want to find out where the note was written, hoping for something like this. So I just looked around in the most likely place."

She said: "Okay. I'll never pretend I know anything again."

They left the place, went back out on the studio street. Ahead of them an outdoor night scene was in progress and heavy flood lamps poured down on some boxes and pilings that were supposed to represent a pier. Vaguely, they could hear the sound of voices, and finally, the clack of the scissors as the camera went into action. They turned in at Marie Dunn's dressing room.

Mickey Ryan was sitting by the corpse smoking a pipe, and the uniformed cop was pacing back and forth. Ryan said: "A guy by the name of Thomas Thurmas called and said you should come to his office. What is he, a big shot or something that he can't come to see you?"

"No," Tony murmured, "he's just small potatoes. He just owns about twenty-five million dollars' worth of stock in this studio is all."

Betty was already on her way back out, and now Tony Key followed her. They moved along a board walk toward the executive offices, both of them silent. Just before they stopped in front of Thurmas' door, Betty broke it. "I don't like it, you going out there to make contact with the kidnapper."

Tony didn't answer, just turned the knob and opened the door, motioning her in. When he was inside he closed the door again. They were standing on a rich black rug facing Thurmas who sat with his fat body squashed in a swivel chair behind a mahogany desk. An armed studio guard stood near him, a black money satchel at his feet.

"I'm sorry for what I said earlier," Thurmas breathed, and Tony could see small beads of perspiration rolling down his fat cheeks. "You'd better go out and pay off the kidnapper and get Marie before something happens to her." He sucked in a wheezing breath, added: "If anything did happen it would be lousy publicity for the studio."

"That's what you're thinking of, isn't it?" said Tony.

"Well, I—I don't like to see anything happen to the kid either."

Betty flounced down in a chair and folded her hands in her lap, waiting. Tony Key glanced at the money satchel, back at the producer. "You can dump all that dough—that forty thousand out on the floor and cover it up with something. Betty's going to stay here with you, and you can keep that guard to see that nothing happens to the money."

"What do you mean?"

"I'm taking an *empty* satchel," Tony said evenly, "my only reason for giving you the instructions I did was to throw off the guilty party, to make him think there was real dough coming. But you producers pay me a lot for doing a good job and I wouldn't risk your forty thousand for the world, Mr. Thurmas. I'm going out there and I hope to bring back both Marie and the killer."

"But you're taking a chance!"

"Maybe."

"I mean on her life, not yours. Marie Dunn's life."

Tony Key smiled thinly. "Then that's my responsibility. That's what I'm hired for. To take responsibilities like that. We've got a nice mob lined up—that carpenter, that red-haired fellow James Turner, the extra Johnny Jones, your director Max White; Kathrine Lewis and Roger Dunn. If it's any of them I think I can handle the situation all right. The only thing on which I could possibly miss is if you yourself are guilty!"

Thomas Thurmas rose to his feet shaking with rage. "*Me* guilty! What motive would I have for— Why would a man in *my* position try to—"

Tony held up his hand. "Never mind. Just dump out the

money and give me the empty satchel."

Thurmas sat down, still sweating, and looking weak. He motioned for the guard to obey Key. Tony waited, then took the satchel and headed for the door. Betty Gale rose silently, blocking him. For a moment Tony stopped, catching her under the elbow and looking down into her pretty upturned face. There was something in the intensity of her gray eyes that made him feel a pulse beat in his throat. He squeezed her arm, said softly, "I'll see you later, honey," and then he was gone, out through the door, the empty satchel in his right hand. He was moving down the board walk.

IT WAS QUITE a distance to the lot where the "Indian Village" had been set up, but he went along with an even step, feeling the night air in his lungs, and the heavy mist in his face, and seeing ahead of him as he reached the outskirts of studio buildings, the swirls of fog-like gray that rose from the Culver hills. He felt his footsteps crunching in the soft, half-wet dirt, and he became conscious suddenly that he was counting his steps, and that there were all kinds of thoughts in his mind, thoughts of past cases, thoughts of the future and always— always that *maybe*. Maybe *this time* I won't come out alive— *Maybe*. There was always that risk, that element of chance, that he might die, and Hollywood would go on without him, with another highest paid detective, and Betty Gale wearing tights and kicking her legs for a musical at Paramet, and all the swell people he had known mentioning him once in awhile and saying "Too bad, wasn't it?"

He thought of these things and then he tried to get them from his mind, he tried to focus down on the present, his mission, his reason, his motive. Always he either led a killer into a trap or, as was the case this time, let the killer lead him into the killer's trap, and this latter, going into the killer's trap, was always more dangerous, for you were going into his ground, playing against his knowledge.

He was soon walking between the tents in the Indian Village, and it was like a miniature town, empty and deserted. Empty as the satchel he held in his hand. The ghosts of red-painted actors walked these streets with him; the echo of clicking cameras of the silent days was in his ears, the thunder of horses hoofs, horses long since gone, the galloping steeds of Tom Mix, and William Farnum, and Bill S. Hart and Harry Cary. They were all here with Tony Key as he walked along.

He arrived at the horse trough, put down the satchel, and leaned against the rusted and waterless tank. Though he leaned against it, he was tense, every muscle keyed to a pitch. His hand moved back to the hip holster—and now he waited. He knew the kidnapper would never let whoever had brought the money out to him go back alive. He knew the game. He was aware that the kidnapper would take no chances on possible future witnesses since he had already murdered once. The second and third murders are nothing, and this one, this killer, had already tasted blood. He would come to shoot Tony, and to take the money. He would release Marie Dunn and she would find her own way back.

Tony waited, knowing this, feeling it instinctively from his knowledge of criminals, and his experience with criminals. He waited in the thick of the starless night knowing it was too dark for him to be a good target. The killer would come up to him as though he was going to take the money, and then he would let him have it.

He suddenly heard a frightened cry. He peered anxiously, holding his gun down at his side so that it could not be seen at once. Then he saw Marie Dunn emerge from the shadows. The little girl's face was a terrified white, her eyes were like big black quarters.

"The man who kidnapped me," she said in a trembling voice, "said that you should give me the money and that I should bring it to him." She recited this like a line from a picture. "He says if you try anything smart he can easily shoot me from where he is, and shoot you too. He says you must give me the money and then wait here for another five minutes."

Tony hissed: "Can he, darling? Can he shoot us from where *he is?*"

"No," she whispered quickly, "he's back in one of those tents waiting."

Tony lifted Marie Dunn, put her in the waterless horse trough, said: "Stay there—stay down," then he plunged forward. But the killer had not remained in the tent. It was only that he had been in the tent when Marie last saw him. For as Tony moved forward bullets rang out.

The staccato whang of the shells roared through the silence, cut a jagged raw-red streak. Tony Key clutched his left arm, was whirled about by the impact of the slug, and then before he realized what was happening, was slamming face-down into the mud. He bit at the mud, jerked his body around, lifted his gun and fired blindly.

Snarling, the killer emerged. He came out of the brush like a charging animal. He was on Tony when Tony was in only a sitting position; still running, the man from the shadows kicked Tony on the side of the head, then stopped, beyond him, whirled about, and brought his gun level. Tony Key, on his hands and knees, his own gun in the dirt, turned to see through the blood that dripped down past his eyes, the muzzle of the killer's automatic pointed straight at his forehead.

6

THERE WAS A moment, the fraction of a second that was eternity, when he waited for the slug to come and split his head wide open; when he waited for the death that he knew he faced each time he went on a case. There was that, and then the instinctive rise to meet the emergency. No fear, for you have no fear while something is happening. Fear is only in waiting for, or looking back, on something. He had no conscious thoughts. His mind telegraphed orders to his body, and the first he knew he was rolling—rolling from the hands and knees position in which he had been.

The shots came simultaneously, but his motion, the rolling motion changed his position and consequently he was not the same target he had been and the bullets missed. He rolled over against the killer's legs, and then he was reaching up, clawing for the gun.

He grabbed the gun wrist, and as he did this he forced his body upward; he braced his legs and forced himself to rise, so that it was like great pressure coming suddenly to bear, and the killer reeled backward with this, unable for the moment to use his gun because Tony had a hold on his wrist.

It was Tony rising with all the strength that was in him to bring himself erect, and the killer being pushed backward. It was all happening in half seconds, the killer going backward, bending back on his heels; now tripping, stumbling backward, sagging, and Tony Key coming down again—coming down on top of the killer this time.

There was that moment when Tony was pressing down, forcing the killer to the earth, when victory seemed sweet and certain, but in pressing him down he lost his grip on the killer's gun, and while he was falling to the earth with him an explosion rocked between them with the shuddering eruption of a volcano.

After that Tony Key's muscles stopped working, everything collapsed within him, and he was sliding off the killer, falling to the ground. He twitched there, fighting to retain consciousness, and retaining it—hearing the footsteps of the frightened killer retreating until these footsteps no longer sounded hollowly in his ears.

Then Tony, with his side bursting with blood was rising, was holding his side. It was only a scratch, the bullet had gone on through. He was rising, his gun still in his hand, strangely, blood beginning to cake on his face where he had been kicked, his left arm hanging limp where it had been shot. He stood there with the night swirling around him, saying:

"Marie… Marie Dunn."

"I'm here," came her voice, "I'm still here. He didn't see me. He just picked up the satchel and ran away."

Tony Key smiled then, his green eyes warm. He turned toward her. "Everything is—all right then."

TONY KEY CAME into Marie Dunn's dressing room all bandaged up, with his left arm in a sling, and his side patched, and a cloth neatly tied about his head. Betty Gale propped him from one side, and little Marie Dunn from the other. He came in and sat down.

"I insist you should be in the hospital," said Betty.

"There'll be time for that later," Tony said, "and I've already got my nurse picked out, too. Only, right now, we have to finish our work, don't we?"

He looked around the room. Bantam Mickey Ryan of Homicide stood there beside his uniformed cop sidekick, waiting. Both of them had their guns out, and handcuffs dangled.

The corpse of Sara Dunn had been removed, but the room was grimly quiet in spite of the number of people who were in it: Thomas Thurmas, the fat, sweating producer who sat in the biggest and most comfortable chair; bald-headed Max White, the director, his shirt still torn, his eyes gleaming; the extra Johnny Jones, muscular and small, and looking frightened; carpenter James Turner, with his red hair, wearing white overalls, looking big and unpleasant. And of course Roger Dunn and Kathrine Lewis.

Tony Key saw them all, looked at them all. Betty Gale was opening her note book.

"The glove," said Tony.

Betty lifted a soiled and bloody heavy white glove from her lap and threw it to the table.

"That was found in the Indian Village after the fray I had there with the killer," he said, "Marie Dunn was blindfolded until she was released to contact me and cannot satisfactorily identify her kidnapper. The glove is court evidence. It is from a pair drawn today from the studio workshop. These gloves are numbered, and the workmen who draw them must sign for them." He looked directly at the large carpenter James Turner. "That establishes the guilt against you quite sufficiently."

The large, red-haired man leapt to his feet. "It's a dirty lie and you know it! You can't put *that* over!"

"Are you denying you drew those gloves today?"

"I drew a pair of gloves—yes!" Turner bellowed.

"Then—"

"It's a frame up, I—"

Tony leapt to his feet. "You *what?*"

James Turner was gulping. "I tell you, I didn't wear them, I—"

"You mean you *didn't wear them when you went to the Indian Village!*"

"That's it, I—"

"But you *did* go to the Indian Village?"

"I—ah—"

Tony rasped: "You *did*, didn't you?"

"I didn't wear the gloves there."

"But you *did* go?"

"Well I—yes, I went. But I didn't wear those gloves and—"

Mickey Ryan and the cop leapt forward and put handcuffs on Turner. He kept raving, but they held him between them. Tony Key sank back down in his chair.

"I was certain of his guilt," he continued as soon as James Turner had subsided, "but I had no evidence. When the cops are sure of somebody they don't mind inventing evidence and convicting with it. I merely invented it to get his admission, through a denial that he had worn the gloves, that he had been to the Indian Village. Nothing infuriates a criminal more than to have a lie told about him. He figures the truth is bad enough. A lie gets him dizzy. It's not a new trick, but you all heard him say he had been there. The way I did it was to take one of his gloves and bloody it up. The gloves were in his locker."

White with rage, James Turner was staring now.

"The actual evidence against him which convinced me of his

guilt," Tony Key went on, "was too slight to present in court. It was the appearance of grease on his overalls. The overalls he had *just put on*, fresh and clean. The position of the places, the color, and the amount of these grease spots, convinced me that he had gotten them from handling the cold cream jar with which Mrs. Sara Dunn was killed. The impact of the blow proved that it was done by a man. These points, along with others—the lack of motive by a man, the poor pay of Turner's job as a carpenter making him a not unlikely kidnapping suspect, and so forth, hung the noose around his neck in the first few moments after I interviewed him, so far as I was concerned."

"Remember, Mr. Turner," Betty Gale said, looking up. "He told you you were crummy. He tipped you off right then."

"Never mind," said Tony, "we have other business. We come now to the motive which wasn't just money. The blotter and cigarette, Betty."

She lifted these items from his pocket and put them on the table.

TONY WENT ON: "Miss Kathrine Lewis, in love with Roger Dunn, wanting to go away with him, maybe to the other end of the world somewhere, but lacking the funds; and bitter about Sara Dunn and his child Marie Dunn, knew that Roger Dunn would never do anything about his predicament, so she planned to have Marie Dunn kidnapped. Obviously, she couldn't do the job alone. She knew James Turner, gave him the proposition, laid out the plan. They would split. With twenty thousand Kathrine and Roger could go away, she figured. Of course Roger Dunn knew nothing about these plans. James

Turner, working only for money, would get the other twenty thousand for doing the dirty work."

Kathrine Lewis rose, her face flushed with anger, and then she sank down in a chair and began to cry. Roger Dunn sat staring straight at Tony Key.

"Miss Lewis had no murder scheduled in this kidnapping. But James Turner evidently suddenly found himself in a position where he had to kill. Sara Dunn probably walked in on him. So he picked up the cold cream jar and let her have it. He snatched little Marie then, left the note that Kathrine Lewis had printed, and made off.

"My evidence against Miss Kathrine Lewis is more concrete, although like all valuable evidence is based on seemingly very simple things. It was these however that led me to the solution. When I took her hand in this room an hour and a half ago it was to look at it more closely. There were faint spots of ink that she had tried desperately to wash off. Remembering how spotty and smudged the kidnap note had been I looked around, found the blotter that had been used, and a cigarette she had smoked while writing it. The cigarette had the pink of the rouge of her mouth on the end of it, and blue spots of ink from her fingers on the sides of it. The blotter, however, handled by her in great haste, has received a perfect fingerprint. This can be compared with her own fingerprint and I am sure you will find it the same. Kathrine figured since Marie Dunn had wrecked, or all but wrecked, Roger Dunn's career, that the money from her kidnapping should be used for them to go away on. She probably reasoned that this was no more than right."

Mickey Ryan moved toward the girl, started to take her wrists.

"Wait a minute," said Tony, and he cast a glance at Thomas Thurmas. The fat producer was wiping sweat from his face with a handkerchief. "Kathrine wasn't on the scene of the murder, neither directed it or had anything to do with it. Since the kidnapping has not been announced outside of this studio the police officially have no authority. That is, they haven't even been told there was a kidnapping. They know there's a murder though, they have the corpse. They *have* to do something about that. But James Turner was in on the murder *alone*. Unless he wishes to involve Kathrine with him as an accomplice and thereby have himself charged with kidnapping as well as murder, I recommend that her part in this be ignored. That's a big request. But I think she's learned the dynamite that is crime and, well—" he shrugged, "it's no longer in my hands."

Kathrine leapt to her feet. "No," she said, "I'm a criminal, and I'll take my punishment."

The fat Thomas Thurmas looked at Roger Dunn. "As Tony says, the kidnapping hasn't been announced, no mention of it will ever be in the papers. It's an affair of the studio. We can press charges or not, as we see fit. The murder is the affair of the police and my carpenter, James Turner, will have to swing for it. But Kathrine's part—the kidnapping—she thought she was doing it for you, and I leave the verdict to you."

Roger Dunn's voice was hoarse. "I'd like to take her in custody," he said, "as my wife, as Marie's new mother."

7

ROGER DUNN STOPPED his car in front of the building on Hollywood Boulevard and told Marie and Kathrine to wait for him a minute. Then he entered the building and went up the stairs. Abe, his agent, had been waiting for him. Poor Abe knew nothing about what had happened and he would never know. Tony Key's cases were like that.

Roger walked along the hall and stopped in front of Abe's door. He paused for a moment. It was still going to be bad news.

He walked in now. The girl at the desk, working long over time, gave him a dirty look and disappeared. She came back a moment later.

"Abe will see you now."

He walked in. Abe was sitting at a big desk.

"I expected you sooner."

"I'm sorry, I—"

"It's all right," Abe raised his hand, let it fall again. "I haven't got anything very happy to tell you. I wanted to tell you personally, and alone. Like this. I thought it would be better than telling Sara. She'll go into hysterics when she hears. She'll try to pawn Marie off on quickies, she'll sell her down the line to two-bit junk shops."

"What do you mean?"

"I mean this, Roger. Marie is through as a child star. She's washed up, finished! Her last two pictures have been duds on the market. They're rushing her through another one but if things go the way they are they'll have to shelve it. It came suddenly. She was a fad. A fad like miniature golf. They're coming back to the old favorites, and you'll have to face it."

Roger could scarcely speak he was so filled with joy, but Abe misinterpreted it for grief.

"It's not going to be so bad," he went on, "if you can get her custody away from Sara and bring her up right. Sara won't be so interested now that she's not worth money, and it shouldn't be so hard. You can be a good father, Roger. In a year Marie will be forgotten by the public and we're going to get you the kind of pictures you should have had at the beginning. Why, on the strength of this I've been able to raise your option to two hundred and fifty a week, and six months from now it'll be three hundred."

But Roger Dunn was not listening now, he was saying in his mind, over and over: the old favorites are coming back, the other was only temporary, only a fad. The real stars are Mickey Mouse and me.

Printed in the USA
CPSIA information can be obtained
at www.ICGtesting.com
JSHW011020101224
75144JS00005B/112